PUFFIN BOOKS

THE PUFFIN BOOK OF INDOOR GAMES

From Cribbage to Crag, Beetle to Battleships, Sebastopol to Sprouts, this marvellous medley of games will appeal to anyone with a sense of fun. While old favourites like Beggar My Neighbour, Boxes and Hangman are included, the more adventurous can try their hands at something new. All the games are graded according to difficulty, with clear, full instructions and helpful diagrams as well as zany cartoons!

Board Games, Match Games, Dice Games, Pencil and Paper Games, Cards and Dominoes make up this stimulating selection and, with seventy-six games in all, there really is something for everyone!

Illustrated by Mike Gordon

Andrew Pennycook

THE PUFFIN BOOK OF

INDOOR GAMES

PUFFIN BOOKS

Puffin Books, Penguin Books Ltd, Harmondsworth, Middlesex, England
Viking Penguin Inc., 40 West 23rd Street, New York, New York 10010, U.S.A.
Penguin Books Australia Ltd, Ringwood, Victoria, Australia
Penguin Books Canada Ltd, 2801 John Street, Markham, Ontario, Canada L3R 1B4
Penguin Books (N.Z.) Ltd, 182–190 Wairau Road, Auckland 10, New Zealand

First published as *The Indoor Games Book* by Faber and Faber Limited 1973
This revised edition first published in Puffin Books 1985
Published simultaneously in hardback by Viking Kestrel

Reproduced, printed and bound in Great Britain by
Hazell Watson & Viney Limited,
Member of the BPCC Group,
Aylesbury, Bucks
Set in 10/12 pt Century Schoolbook by
Rowland Phototypesetting Ltd, Bury St Edmunds, Suffolk

For Margaret, Veronica, Francis and Rosemary

CONTENTS

The simplest games have no asterisk. The number of asterisks increases with the complexity of the game. The number of players is given in brackets.

2   DOMINO GAMES   90

3 BOARD GAMES 118

4 DICE GAMES 161

INTRODUCTION

The games in this book are described fully so that you will be able to follow the instructions and play the games with understanding. In general, the easier games are given at the beginning of each section; an asterisk (*) after the title of a game means it is more difficult and the hardest of all have two asterisks (**). Do not neglect a game because it can be played by children younger than yourself – many of them can be played by young children but older children can play them better and with more enjoyment. After all, chess can be played by eight-year-old children but many adults spend their whole lives playing it.

In using the book to learn a new game everybody should get together round the table so that they can all listen to the rules. All games are more fun to play if you keep to the rules and this is the easiest way of making sure that everybody knows them. Another good idea is to play the game once 'just to see how it goes' since this means you can settle differences before you start playing properly.

You may find that you know a different way of playing some of the games I have described, or you may have a favourite game which I have not written about. If this is so I should be pleased to get a letter from you describing it – you never can tell but it may be included in a later edition.

Lastly, I hope you will enjoy learning the games in this book but please remember that games are played for fun; never try to make a loser feel silly, or boast too much if you have won – you may only have done so because of luck.

ANDREW PENNYCOOK

1 CARD GAMES

All the games in this section of the book are played with an ordinary pack of cards. These can be bought in any stationer's or newsagent's shop and are probably one of the best 'games' that you can buy. This section has only some of the games that can be played with a pack of cards so you can see how many there must be. The game you play can be for any number of people from one to a houseful; and the games can be as easy as *Slap-jack* or as difficult as *Cribbage* – there is something for everyone in a pack of cards.

When you are playing most card games you pick up the cards that have been given to you, turn them so that you can see what their values and suits are, spread them out like a fan and look at them. This is where the numbers and letters in the corners of the cards come in useful. You can easily tell which cards you have got just by looking at the corners and you should arrange your fan of cards so that you can see the corners easily without worrying about seeing what is on the face of the cards.

In some games it is best to arrange your cards so that all those of the same suit are together. But be careful before doing this because in some games it is important to keep your cards mixed together so that your opponent cannot guess which ones are high or low.

Drawing for dealer

All these games need someone to be the dealer (the person who gives out the cards to the other players) or the first player. There are nearly as many ways of choosing this person as there are card games, but I will describe one which is very easy and very good. It is called 'drawing for dealer'. The pack of cards is mixed together, by shuffling in the hands or on the table, and is then spread out face downwards across the table so that the cards are in a line, overlapping each other. Each player picks out one card and, when all have done so, these cards are turned face up. The player with the highest card wins and becomes either the dealer or the first player.

If two players have cards of the same pip value then a spade beats a heart, a heart beats a diamond, a diamond beats a club. The aces count as higher than kings.

So that if the ace of clubs and the ace of spades were taken from the pack the player who got the ace of spades would win. If the 9 of diamonds and the 6 of hearts were drawn, the player with the 9 of diamonds would win.

It is best not to take cards from the last five at either the top or bottom of the pack but to choose cards from the middle. This stops certain kinds of cheating.

Another way of choosing the first dealer is for anyone to give out the cards, one at a time from the top of the pack and face up, to each player going round the table in order to the left all the time. The first player to be given a jack is the dealer. Another is for anyone to give out one card to each player and the player with the highest card is the winner.

Some people like to count aces low instead of high in choosing the dealer and some ignore the differences between the suits so that two players drawing cards of the same pip value will tie. In this case the players who have tied are made to choose again to see which of them wins.

It does not matter which way you use of choosing a dealer so long as everyone who is going to play knows how you are going to do it. Arguments can start very easily if someone draws an ace and expects to win only to be told 'Oh, no, aces are low.' Before you draw for dealer state the rules – 'Aces high, highest deals' or 'Aces low, highest deals' and so on. In that way no one can say afterwards that you have cheated.

Shuffling

Many people find shuffling difficult – they drop the cards, or get them facing both ways – even when they try the overhand shuffle. To do this properly you hold the pack upright in one hand, usually the right, with the cards all facing away from you. It is easiest to hold the cards at the ends between the thumb and two middle fingers. Hold your other hand below the pack with the fingers sloping up. You then let a small packet of cards slide off the top of the pack and catch it in your other hand so that the cards lean against your fingers.

When you have done this, you let another small packet drop on top of the first and keep on doing this until the whole pack is in your other hand. You should shuffle the cards like this several times before beginning a new deal.

If you find this too difficult you can try this other way of mixing the cards together. Gather the cards up in any order, making sure that they are all facing in the same direction. Then deal three cards some little distance apart, face down. On top of these deal three more cards and a fourth card beside them. The next time deal five cards, then six, and lastly seven.

When you have seven piles you start dealing in the opposite direction: first putting out two cards (one on the right-hand pile and the other on the pile next to it), then putting out three cards (on the right-hand pile, the pile next to it and the third pile from the right) and so on, increasing the number of cards given at each deal by one until you have used up all the cards.

The piles are gathered up in any order you like to make the pack for the next deal. Of course, you can do this shuffle several times if you want to.

The deal

When the dealer is chosen the player on his right (or the other player if there are only two) shuffles the cards and hands them to him. The dealer gives out the cards one at a time to each player going round the table clockwise, that is to his left. The cards are given out face down so that no one can see their values. In some games the cards have to be given out two or three at a time.

If the dealer makes a mistake in giving out the cards, either giving two cards to one player by mistake, or finding a card face up in the pack, or accidentally turning one over in putting it on the table, all the cards are gathered together, reshuffled by the player on the dealer's right, and given out again by the same dealer.

If you find after all the cards have been given out that some players have too many and some too few, it is usual for those with too few to pick the extra cards from the hands of those with too many. Naturally without looking at the faces of the cards.

Card games, like all games, are fun to play but you must learn to play by some set of rules that everyone knows. If you do not do this you will spend more time arguing about the rules than you will in enjoying the game. So decide what you are going to play, and how you are going to play it, before you start and don't change your mind half-way through.

SLAP-JACK   *Two or more players*

An exciting game that does not need any understanding of cards except the ability to recognize the jacks.

An old pack of cards is used – the older the better – and it does not really matter if one or two cards are missing.

The object of the game is to win cards by touching jacks every time they appear.

All the cards are given out, one at a time, face down, going round to the left. It does not matter if some players have one more card than the others.

The cards are kept in piles, face down, in front of each player. No one must look at the faces of their cards.

The player on the dealer's left turns over the top card of his pile and puts it face up in the middle of the table. All the other players, in turn going round to the left, do exactly the same, putting their cards on top of those that have already been played.

Every time a jack appears, the first player to slap it or lay his hand on it, wins all the cards in the pile. If more than one player has touched the jack the player whose hand is underneath all the others is the winner. It is a good idea to have a referee who can settle any arguments.

If you touch a card that is not a jack you must give a card to the player who put it out on the pile.

When you win the pile of cards by slapping a jack, you pick up the whole pile, turn it over and put it with your face-down pile. You then shuffle this new pile.

This shuffled pile becomes your new face-down pile. The player on your left turns over his top card and starts a new face-up pile in the middle of the table.

A player who has no more cards is out of the game, except that he can try to slap the next jack. If he slaps this jack before anyone else he can carry on with his new pile, but if he does not he is out of the game.

The player who stays in longest and collects all the cards is the winner.

MENAGERIE   *Three or more players*

A happy, noisy game which becomes more enjoyable the larger the number of players.

You need an ordinary pack of cards for up to six players. If there are more than six players shuffle two or more packs together and use them as one large pack.

First of all everyone who is going to play thinks of the name of an animal. The longer the name the better the chance of winning and it is probably best for each player to be given a small piece of paper on which he writes the name of an animal. The pieces of paper are then shaken up in a hat or a bag and the players take it in turn to pull one piece of paper out of the hat. The name on this piece of paper will be theirs for the game. You must be careful that everybody has different animal names.

When everyone knows everybody else's names, the fifty-two cards of the pack are given out one at a time, face down, going round to the left, until there are no more left. It does not matter if some players have one more card than the others. The players do not look at their cards but put them face down on the table in front of them in a neat pile.

The object of the game is to win all the cards.

Suppose the four players are Margaret, Veronica, Francis and Rosemary and that Margaret's animal is

Chimpanzee, Veronica's is Hippopotamus, Francis's is Elephant and Rosemary's is Rhinoceros. Let them sit round a table like this:

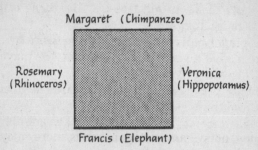

Margaret (Chimpanzee)

Rosemary (Rhinoceros)

Veronica (Hippopotamus)

Francis (Elephant)

Margaret dealt out the cards, so Veronica turns up the top card of her pile to start the game. Suppose it is a 9 (this game does not bother about suits).

Francis, on Veronica's left, quickly turns over his top card, but it is a 5 so he does nothing.

Rosemary, on Francis's left, turns over her top card – and it is a 9, matching Veronica's card. It is then a race between the two of them to see who first can call out the other's animal name three times. So while Rosemary struggles with saying 'Hippopotamus, hippopotamus, hippopotamus', Veronica is trying to say 'Rhinoceros, rhinoceros, rhinoceros'. The one that finishes first is the winner and takes all the face-up cards of the other. The winner puts these cards, *face down*, at the bottom of his pile. The player on the winner's left then starts the next round by turning up the top card of his pile.

Play goes on like this, always passing to the left, and the players take it in turn to turn up the top cards of their face-down piles and put them on top of their face-up piles so that only one card can be seen on each pile at a time. And every time that anyone turns up a card that matches the top card of someone else's pile, the two players race to call each other's animal name three times.

When a player runs out of cards in his face-down pile, he simply picks up his face-up pile, turns it over and goes through it again.

If a player calls out a name three times by mistake, he must give all his face-up cards to the player whose name he called.

When a player has lost all his cards he is out of the game and the others carry on.

At last only two players are left, then one of them gets all the cards and wins the game.

You may find that the last two players keep on playing and playing without anyone winning so that everyone else gets tired of watching them. The best way to stop this is to set a limit – they can only play ten or fifteen rounds – and when they have finished the player who has the most cards is the winner.

BEGGAR MY NEIGHBOUR   *Two or more players*

One of the easiest games, *Beggar My Neighbour* needs no skill but the way the cards move backwards and forwards is the cause of much amusement.

The object of the game is to win all the cards.

The dealer gives out all the cards, one at a time face down, going round to the left. It does not matter if some players have one more card than the others.

Each player puts his cards in a neat pile in front of him, face down. You do not look at your cards.

The player on the dealer's left turns up the top card of his pile and puts it face up in the middle of the table. Each player in turn, going round to the left, puts a card on top of the central pile until one of them turns up an ace, king, queen or jack.

For an ace the next player must turn up four cards; for a king, three cards; for a queen, two cards; and for a jack, one card. But he stops turning over cards if he turns up an ace, king, queen or jack and the next player on his left is forced to turn over cards in the same way, and so on round the table.

The turn goes on until someone does not turn over an ace, king, queen or jack among the cards he is forced to play. When this happens the player who put out the last ace, king, queen or jack takes all the cards in the pile, turns them over and puts them at the bottom of his own pile.

For example, suppose Margaret puts down the ace of spades. Veronica, who is next, has four chances to put down a card and not lose the pile. Suppose Veronica's first three cards are the 7 of clubs, the 9 of spades and the 4 of hearts. She has only one chance left and is very happy to turn up the king of diamonds.

Now it is Francis's turn and he has three chances of not losing the pile. His first card is the 10 of diamonds, so he has to turn up the next one. It is the queen of hearts and he does not have to worry any more. Rosemary has two chances of not losing the pile and she is lucky with her first card – it is the jack of clubs.

Margaret, however, only has one chance of saving the pile. She turns her card, finds it is the 5 of clubs and Rosemary wins the whole pile. Of course, if Margaret had turned up an ace, king, queen or jack the turn would have passed to Veronica and so on round the table until someone failed to pass it on.

You will see that the jacks are stronger than aces because the next player has only one chance with a jack but he has four chances with an ace. So you are more likely to pick up the pile if you put up a jack than an ace.

When a player has picked up the pile, he puts out the top card from the pile in his hand, face up in the middle of the table as the first card for a new pile. Play goes round to the left as before.

A player who lost all his cards is out of the game.

The player who first collects all fifty-two cards is the winner.

Some people find that the game lasts too long when there are only two people left in. Try playing *Beggar My Neighbour* with a thirty-two-card piquet pack (no 2s, 3s, 4s, 5s or 6s). This makes the game much faster.

If you find a thirty-two-card pack is too quick, try putting back the 6s, or the 6s and the 5s, until you get a pack of the right size to give you a game you like.

DONKEY *Three or more players (best with five or six)*

Donkey is a splendid, fast, noisy game which is enjoyed by everyone.

Sort out the pack into sets of cards each with four cards of the same value – four aces, four 5s, four queens and so on. Use as many sets of four as there are players. If there are five players you could use the aces, 2s, 3s, 4s and 5s. For six players you add the 6s; for four players you take away the 5s.

The object of the game is to collect four cards of the same value while watching out that you do not get caught as donkey.

The cards are shuffled and are dealt out, one card at a time, face down, to each player, going round to the left. It does not matter which player deals.

The players pick up their cards and look at them. They each choose one card from their hands and they put this card face down on the table to their left. Each player then picks up the card he has been given by the player on his right, puts it in his hand, chooses another card he does not want (it can be the card he has just picked up) and puts it on the table to his left. This passing is kept up as quickly as possible, each player hoping that he will get four cards of the same value before anybody else does.

As soon as any player gets four cards all the same, he puts them down quietly on to the table and puts one finger along the side of his nose. When another player sees this he also puts his cards down – even if he does not have four of a kind – and places *his* finger alongside his nose. At last everybody will see what is happening and they will all put down their cards. The last player to get his finger to his nose is the 'donkey' for that round.

The first person to have been donkey six times is the loser. The score is kept most easily by writing everybody's names down in a column on a piece of paper. Each time a player loses he gets one letter of the word *donkey* written opposite his name and the first person to get the whole word is the loser.

Another way of discovering the donkey for each round is to put out some buttons or beans in the middle of the table. Of course you make sure that the number of buttons is one less than the number of people playing – five beans for six players and so on.

Whenever a player puts down his cards because he has got four of a kind, all the players grab for the buttons. The player who does not get a button is donkey for the round.

SNIP-SNAP-SNOREM *Three or more players*

A very old game which is still enjoyed, both because it is so simple and because everyone has something to do.

You use an ordinary pack of cards.

A dealer is chosen by drawing cards as described on p. 14 and the cards are shuffled.

The dealer gives out all the cards, face down, one at a time, to all the players going round to the left until all the cards have been given out. It does not matter if some players have one card more than the others.

The players each pick up the cards in front of them and look at them.

The player on the dealer's left puts out any card he likes, face up, in the middle of the table. Suppose it is a 9. The player on his left must put out a 9 if he has one, saying 'Snip'. If he does not have a 9 he says 'Pass' and the player on his left has his turn. Players, in turn, keep saying 'Pass' until one of them is able to put out a 9 and say 'Snip'.

The next player has to put out the third 9, saying 'Snap', or has to say 'Pass'. After the third card has been played, the player who puts out the fourth 9 has to say 'Snorem'. He can then start a new round with any card he likes, and play goes on as before.

Some people say that you can put out the cards one at a time if you have more than one of the same value. Suppose you have two 5s. You put one of them out and by the time it gets back to your turn the last player should have said 'Snap'. You can then put out your second 5, say 'Snorem' and start the next round.

Other people say that if you have two 5s you must put them both out when it is your turn. If you are starting the round, you put out one of them and then the second and say 'Snip'. If it is the middle of the round you put out the first and say 'Snip', for example, and then the second and say 'Snap'.

I think the first way is better but you can try both to see which you like.

The first player to get rid of all his cards is the winner.

FISH *Three to six players*

This game is great fun, especially for young children since they are often able to beat the grown ups without being helped.

You need an ordinary pack of cards.

The object of the game is to collect sets of four cards of the same value.

The dealer is chosen by drawing as described on p. 14. After the player on his right has shuffled, the dealer gives out five cards to each player, one at a time, face down, going round to the left. The cards which are left over at the end of the deal are placed face down in the middle of the table.

The player on the left of the dealer asks any other player for a particular card, by suit and value – the 6 of hearts, say, or the queen of clubs. You can only ask for a card if you have one of the same value in your hand. If the player gets the card he asked for, he can ask for another card, either from the same player or from another one, just as he pleases.

When he asks a player for a card that player does not have, he gets the answer 'Fish' and has to take the top card from the pile in the middle. The player who answered 'Fish' then takes up the job of asking for cards.

Every time a player manages to collect four cards of the same value, he shows them to the other players, and puts them face down in a neat pile in front of him.

The winner is the first person to get rid of all his cards but, if more than one person is out at the same time, the winner is the player with most sets of four in front of him.

CHEAT   *Three or more players (best with more than four)*

This game is very popular, especially when it is understood that to play it well you have to lie without being found out. It is best played quickly without long gaps between the players taking their turns.

The game is usually played with the full pack of fifty-two cards but I have found that it goes on for too long with young children. With them I use a smaller pack, throwing out the 2s, 3s, 4s, 5s and 6s to make the thirty-two-card pack, or the jacks, queens and kings to make a forty-card pack.

If you are going to play with more than five people you may find the game is too short with one pack and you can use two packs shuffled together.

The dealer is chosen by drawing cards as described on p. 14 and gives out all the cards, one at a time, face down, to each player going round the table to the left. It does not matter if some players have one more card than others.

After the cards have been given out the players pick them up and look at them. The player on the dealer's left then chooses one of his cards, puts it *face down* on the table, being careful not to let anyone see what it is, and names a value. He can of course say the real value of the card but he does not have to. In fact he says the value that he wants everybody else to think it is. He does not have to tell the truth.

The player on his left then puts out one card from his hand, saying it is of the next higher value. Suppose the first player has said '10', the second player has to put out a card and call it 'Jack' whether it is or not.

The next player puts out a 'Queen', the next a 'King', then an 'Ace', '2', and so on. Everybody should play as quickly as possible.

If you have taken out some cards to make the pack smaller, you must remember to jump the gap. In the thirty-two-card pack the 7 follows the ace; in the forty-card pack the ace follows the 10.

At any time any of the players can call out 'Cheat' if they think that someone has not put out a card of the value they have said for the top card of the face-down pile. When 'Cheat' is called the card is turned over so that everyone can see it.

If it is what the player said it was (a 4 if he said '4') the player who called 'Cheat' has to pick up all the cards from the middle of the table and put them in his hand. The player he challenged puts out the first card for the next round.

If the player had in fact cheated (put out a 10, and said '4') then he has to pick up all the cards from the middle of the table and put them in his hand. The player who correctly called 'Cheat' puts out the first card for the next round.

If more than one player calls out 'Cheat' at the same time, the player sitting nearest to the challenged player's left hand is taken to be the first. This stops a lot of arguments.

The first player to get rid of all his cards is the winner.

For a more thrilling game you can put out one, two, three or four cards at a time. You must not put out fewer cards than the player before you, but you can put out more if you like. The values claimed by players must go up in steps of one as for the simple form of *Cheat*. For example, Veronica may put out 'Two 3s' (or pretend she has), Rosemary then says that she has put out 'Two 4s', Francis claims 'Three 5s' and Margaret tries 'Four 6s'. Naturally the cards you put out do not all have to be the same – you just say they are.

Just as in the simple game the value of the cards put out must be in order – kings following queens, aces following kings, and so on. And as in the other game, anyone can say 'Cheat' whenever they like but if they are wrong they have to collect all the cards that have been played.

MY SHIP SAILS   *Three to seven players*

This is an excellent game, even for people who know nothing about cards.

You need an ordinary pack of cards.

The object of the game is to collect seven cards of the same suit – seven clubs, seven diamonds, seven hearts or seven spades.

The dealer is chosen by drawing as described on p. 14. After the player on his right has shuffled, the dealer gives out seven cards, one at a time, face down, to each player, going round to the left. Any cards that are left over are put face down in the middle of the table and are not used.

Each player picks up the cards in front of him and looks at them. He then chooses one of his cards and puts it, *face down*, on the table to his left. Suppose you have three spades, two hearts, a diamond and a club. You will probably think that you should collect spades or hearts, and will put out either the diamond or the club.

When everybody has put out a card to the left, each player picks up the card on his right. That is each player passes a card to the player on his left.

Everybody looks at their hands again and if they do not have seven cards of the same suit, they each choose a card from their hand and put it face down on the table to their left before picking up the card that has been passed to them.

The first player to collect seven cards of the same suit shouts 'My ship sails', and puts his cards face up on the table. He is the winner of the game.

If two players find they have seven cards of the same suit in their hands at the same time, the winner is the one who first started to shout.

Most of the fun in this game comes when two, or more, players are trying to collect the same suit. This always happens when five or more people play and so the game is best for the larger number.

CUCUMBER   *Three players*

A game for three players which was first shown me by David Parlett, although I understand he learnt it from John McLeod, who I hope will not object to my describing it here.

The object of the game is to end up with the lowest-value card at the table. At the end of the game the cards rise in value from the aces to the kings.

You can use either a fifty-two-card pack or the smaller thirty-two-card piquet pack (all the cards from the 7s to the aces).

The dealer is chosen as described on p. 14, and he shuffles the cards and deals six cards to each player, one at a time, face down. The remaining cards are put to one side and are not used during the hand.

The player on the dealer's left chooses one card from his hand and places it face up in the middle of the table. Each player in turn has to put out a card of equal or greater value. Suits do not count and the aces are high in play (so that the cards go up in value from the 2s to the aces). If a player cannot equal or beat the top card played, he must play his lowest-value card.

The trick is won by the player who put out the card of the highest value. He leads to the next trick. If two or more cards of equal value are played, the first one played counts as the highest.

When five tricks have been played, each player shows the card he is left with and the player with the lowest card (remember aces are low for this) scores the sum of the cards in the other players' hands. For this jacks count 11, queens 12 and kings 13; all the others have their pip values.

Should two players have cards of the same value, they each score the value of the card in the hand of the remaining player.

The deal passes anti-clockwise round the table and the game continues until one player has reached an agreed target (usually 50 or 100).

CRAZY EIGHTS *Two to eight players*

An enjoyable game which is probably best for two, three or four players.

You use an ordinary pack of fifty-two cards if two, three or four people are playing. If there are more than four, use two ordinary packs shuffled together.

The object of the game is to get rid of all your cards.

The dealer is chosen by drawing as described on p. 14 and the player on his right shuffles the pack.

The dealer gives out seven cards to each player, one at a time, face down, going round to the left. The remainder of the pack is placed face down in the middle of the table and is called the *stock*. The top card of the stock is turned face up and is placed beside the pile. This card is called the *starter*.

Each player picks up the cards in front of him and looks at them.

The player on the dealer's left then chooses a card from his hand which is either of the same suit as the starter or is of the same value. If the starter is the 3 of diamonds, he must play a 3 or a diamond.

If he does not want to follow suit or value, or if he cannot follow suit or value, he can play an 8 of any suit — if he has one. 8s are 'wild', which means they can be any suit you like to name. When you play an 8, you must say which suit it represents and the next player must put out either a card of that suit or another 8. You can call any suit you like when you put out an 8, and the other players must pretend it is an 8 of that suit.

If a player cannot follow suit or value, and does not have an 8, he must take cards, one at a time, off the top of the stock and put them with the other cards in his hand until he draws a card he can play, or all the cards have been taken from the stock. If there are no cards left in the stock the player must pass if he cannot play.

When the player on the dealer's left has had his turn and has put out a card on top of the starter, the next player on his left has his turn. He must play a card of the same suit or value as the top card of the starter pile, or play an 8 and name any suit he likes.

Play goes on like this, always passing round the table to the left, until one player manages to get rid of all his cards.

Each player then shows the cards remaining in his hand and the winner scores fifty points for each 8 that is held, ten points for each ace, king, queen or jack, and the pip value for all the others. If the game has ended because no one can play, the player with the lowest score wins but the points in his hand are taken away from the total of the points held by the other players.

The first player to reach a given total, say 500 points, is the winner.

It is important to realize that you can take cards from

the stock even though you are able to follow suit or value or have an 8 in your hand. This may be to your advantage, especially early in the game when it is not a good idea to play an 8. 8s become more and more powerful as the game goes on and you can sometimes force an opponent to pick up all the cards in the stock by playing the last 8 and naming a suit that has been played out.

Do not think that having more cards than your opponent is always a disadvantage. If you have any idea which cards he is holding you can often get rid of all your cards without letting him get rid of any.

Crazy Eights is sometimes played with the thirty-two-card piquet pack (no 2s, 3s, 4s, 5s or 6s) and a joker. The joker is just like the 8s – it can always be played on anything and can be called any suit you please. In this game (for two or four) you deal five cards to each player.

Some people play with the 9s 'wild' (*Neuner*) and others with the aces 'wild' (*Rockaway*). All these games are exactly the same except for different wild cards.

PARLIAMENT   *Three or more players*

This game is also called *Sevens* and *Card Dominoes* and is related to *Crazy Eights*.

You need only one pack of cards if any number from three to eight is playing but, for more than eight, it is best to shuffle two packs together.

The object of the game is to get rid of your cards as quickly as possible.

The dealer is chosen by drawing as described on p. 14 and the player on his right shuffles the pack.

The dealer then gives out all the cards, one at a time to each player, face down, going round to the left. It does not matter if some players have one more card than the others.

Each player picks up the cards in front of him and looks at them.

The player on the dealer's left chooses any card from his hand and places it face up in the middle of the table. The next player on his left must play either the next higher or the next lower card in the same suit, or a card of the same value as the first card. For example, if the first player put out the 6 of clubs, the second player can put out either the 5 or the 7 of clubs, or any other 6.

Sequences end at the ace at the bottom and the king at the top. An ace cannot be put on a king and a king cannot be put on an ace.

If a player cannot go he must pass.

Play passes to the left round the table with each player either adding one card to one of the sequences, or playing a card of the same value as the first card, or passing.

The winner is the first player to get rid of all his cards.

Although this game is very simple, that does not mean you do not have to pay attention to the cards that have been played. You should look at the cards in your hand and try to work out which ones will give you the best chances of playing next time round, and which ones will give your opponents the fewest chances of playing.

Suppose you could play the 6 of diamonds or the 8 of clubs. If you have the 9 and 10 of clubs in your hand it is obviously better to put out the 8 of clubs so that you can get rid of the 9 and 10 on your next two turns. This also means that you are keeping the 6 of diamonds out of play, which must annoy at least one of your opponents.

Of course, you do not have to play the 10 of clubs on top of the 9 at your first chance. If you can play any other card it is probably better to do so, blocking your opponents on the 10.

TRICKS *Two to thirteen players*

While as many as thirteen can play *Tricks* it is good for any smaller number.

Each person is given four cards. The youngest player is asked to put out his highest card face up in the middle of the table. All the other players in turn, going round to the left, then have to play a card of the same *suit* on top of this card. If they have no cards of this suit they can put out any card from the other suits in their hands. If a player does not follow suit the next player still has to play a card of the same suit as the first player if he can. He does not play a card of the same suit as the one that was thrown away.

When each player has put out one card, you stop playing for the moment and look to see who has *won the trick*. The player who put out the highest card of the same suit as that which was put out by the first player is said to have *won the trick*. He gathers together all the cards that have been played on to the table, and puts them in a neat pile, face down, in front of him. This pile is a 'trick'. He then chooses one of his cards and puts it out on to the table face up as the first card of a new trick. The other players follow suit if they can or throw away a card. The winner of this trick leads to the next and so on until none of the players have any cards left and all four tricks have been won.

The player with the most tricks in front of him is the winner.

When you are choosing which cards to throw away remember that it is best to throw away low ones. Jacks, queens and kings might win tricks later on, while 2s and 3s will not.

The first few times that you play this game you will probably find that it is easiest to have the aces as low cards and the kings as the highest. But as the players get to know the game you can change the rules.

The first change is to make the aces high.

Then choose a suit for trumps. The easiest way to choose trumps is to go through the suits in order – having spades as trumps for the first round, hearts for the second, diamonds the third, clubs the fourth and then starting again with spades. Another good way is to give out the four cards to each player and put the next card face up in the middle of the table. Cards of the same suit as this are trumps.

Any card in the trump suit beats any other card except a higher trump. For example, suppose hearts are trumps. The 2 of hearts will beat the ace of spades or the 9 of diamonds or the 3 of clubs. But the 2 of hearts will be beaten by any other heart. You are not usually allowed to play a trump unless you do not have any cards in the suit that was led, that is unless you would have been throwing away a card. Of course, if trumps are led you have to play a trump if you have one and the winning card is the highest trump in the trick.

Once you understand how to play with trumps you can start giving the players more than four cards each. Before you know where you are you will be playing *Whist*.

ROLLING STONE* *Four, five or six players*

This is a very amusing game which can last for a long time. Young children enjoy it because of the way in which the cards roll backwards and forwards from one hand to another. At one minute you have nearly won, at the next you have a handful of cards.

Before you start you must make sure that there are only enough cards in the pack to give each player eight. If four people are playing you use a piquet pack (no 2s, 3s, 4s, 5s or 6s); for five players you use a forty-card pack (no 2s, 3s or 4s); for six people you use a forty-eight-card pack (no 2s).

The object of the game is to get rid of your cards as quickly as possible.

Choose a dealer by drawing cards as described on p. 14. After the player on the dealer's right has shuffled them, the dealer gives the cards out, one at a time, face down, to each player, going round the table to his left until he has given out all the cards.

The players pick up their cards and look at them. Then the player on the dealer's left chooses a card from his hand and puts it face up in the middle of the table.

Each player in turn must put out a card of the same suit if he can.

If all the players have been able to put out a card of the same suit as the first card played, the player who put out the highest card of that suit has won the 'trick'. He gathers the cards from the middle of the table, puts them in a neat pile and puts them, face down, in front of him. They take no further part in the game. The winner of the trick then chooses any card from his hand, and puts it face up in the middle of the table and play goes on as before.

If any player does not have any cards of the suit led he must pick up all the cards that have been played to the trick and put them in his hand. He then chooses any card from another suit and puts it face up in the middle of the table as the first card of the next trick. For example if he does not have a spade and has to pick up several spades, his next lead must be a heart, a club or a diamond.

There are no trumps in this game and you must follow suit if you can.

The winner is the first player to get rid of all his cards.

COMMIT*   *Two or more players (the more the better)*

Commit was invented in France at a time when a comet was very prominent in the sky. The people believed that this meant the end of the world – a stop to everything – and the stops in this game poke fun at this.

You use an ordinary pack of cards but take out the 8 of diamonds and put it away safely.

The object of the game is to get rid of all your cards.

The dealer is chosen by drawing as described on p. 14. After the player on his right has shuffled the cards, the dealer gives them out one at a time, face down, to each player until he does not have enough left to go right round. These remaining cards are put in the middle of the table, face down, and are not used for the game.

Each player picks up the cards in front of him and looks at them.

The player on the dealer's left chooses a card from his hand and puts it face up in the middle of the table. As he does so he names its value. If he puts out the 6 of hearts he says 'Six'. If he has the 7 of hearts he puts it out on top of the 6, and says 'Seven'. If he has the 8 of hearts he puts it out and says 'Eight'. If he does not have the 8 he says 'Without the eight' and the player on his left has a chance to put the 8 on top of the pile.

Of course, if he too does not have the 8 he has to say 'Without the eight' and the player on his left has a turn and so on round the table.

You must put out as many cards as you can when it is your turn.

It may happen that no one has the next card in their hands because it is among the face-down cards in the middle of the table (or it is the 8 of diamonds). This means that the turn passes right round the table and back to the player who put out the last card. You have found a 'stop' and the player who led the last card puts out any other card he likes to start a new pile.

The kings are called 'natural stops' and whenever a player puts a king on top of a pile (on top of a queen of the same suit) he is allowed to put out any other card he likes to start a new sequence.

If you have the 9 of diamonds in your hand you can put it out to start a new sequence whenever it is your turn to play. You do not have to put the next card on the sequence that is going but can put out your 9 of diamonds to start a new one. The next player on your left can then, when you have finished putting out as many cards as you can, put out cards on top of the old sequence or on top of the 9 of diamonds (or the top diamond you have left).

The first player to get rid of all his cards is the winner.

RACING DEMON*   *Two or more players*

A noisy, fast game for any number of players which does not need any skill, just speed at seeing how you can get rid of some of your cards.

You need one ordinary pack of cards for each player and it is best to use the oldest cards you have because they will probably be bent or torn in a really rough game. The packs should have different backs, so that you can tell them apart easily.

It is best if the players sit round a large table with their cards in front of them. There should be plenty of room in the middle of the table. Make sure that the younger players can reach out into the middle easily before you start playing.

At the beginning each player has his pack face down in front of him, properly shuffled. When everybody is ready each one deals out thirteen cards face down in a pile in front of himself and then turns them over so that only the top card can be seen. They also deal out four cards, face up and side by side, to make a row beside the pile. The remaining cards are held face down in one hand.

One of the players is chosen as starter and when he

sees that everybody is ready he shouts 'Go' and the scramble begins.

Each player plays for himself as quickly as he can. There are no turns and the fastest player usually wins.

At the word 'Go' each player takes any aces that are face up in his cards, whether in the row of four or on top of his pile, and puts them face up in the middle of the table.

As soon as an ace is put down in the middle of the table *anyone* who has a 2 of the same suit can put it on top of the ace. It does not have to come from the same pack. As soon as the 2 is on, a 3 can be played and so on until the king is reached.

Once a player has put out a card from his row he fills the gap with the top card from his pile of thirteen. The player can also put the cards in the row on top of each other in order of value but changing colour with each card – an alternating sequence. You can also move a card from the pile on to a sequence but you cannot build up a sequence on top of the face-up pile.

For example you might have the cards laid out like this:

Face-up row   Face-up pile

You put the ace of spades in the middle of the table, move the 8 of hearts into the row, put the 7 of spades (a *black* 7) on top of the 8 of hearts (a *red* 8), the 6 of diamonds (a *red* 6) on top of the 7 of spades (a *black* 7) and the 5 of clubs (a *black* 5) on top of the 6 of diamonds (a *red* 6). This leaves you with three gaps in your row and you fill these with the top three cards from the face-up pile.

You now move any cards you can from this new row into the piles growing in the middle of the table, or on to each other.

Only the smallest card can be taken off a sequence. In the example above you have to get rid of the 5 of clubs before you can put out the 6 of diamonds.

If you get the chance to move a whole sequence on top of a card, you can do so, but you must move all the cards in the sequence. For example, if a black 9 appears in the row above, you can put the whole sequence (8♡–7♠–6◇–5♣) on to it but you are not allowed to move part of a sequence (like 6◇–5♣) even though the 7 of clubs is free.

After you have played like this for a little while you will find that you are 'stuck' and cannot put out any more cards or move them on to new sequences. As soon as this happens you turn over the top three cards of the pile held in the hand and place them face up in a neat pile in front of you so that you can see the top card only. If the top card is an ace or can be put on one of the piles in the middle you play it; if it fits on top of one of your sequences you play it there. Of course, if you can make gaps in your row you do so to let you get rid of cards from the face-up pile.

If you still cannot play you turn over the next three cards and put them on top of the first three. You keep on doing this until you can play. If you run out of cards you pick up the stack you have just dealt, turn it over, and start again.

The game has two objects and you must remember both of them.

Firstly you are trying to get rid of all the cards in the

face-up pile of thirteen cards (either by playing them on to your row of four or out into the middle).

Secondly you are trying to put as many cards as possible out into the middle.

When one of the players has got rid of all the thirteen cards in his face-up pile he calls 'Out' and everybody stops playing immediately.

The cards in the middle of the table are picked up and sorted out (this is why you have to be able to tell the packs apart easily) and put in front of their owners.

Each player's score is the number of cards he put out into the middle of the table less the number of cards left in his face-up pile. A player who has put out nineteen cards into the middle of the table, but has three cards left in his face-up pile scores sixteen points (19 − 3 = 16). Some people give the first player to get rid of his thirteen cards ten points and they also give ten points to each player who puts out a king. This makes the game even faster.

If you are going to play *Racing Demon* it is a good idea to have a referee who can sort out any fights that start. A referee is essential if there is a large number of players. The referee should not try to play as well as keep the peace – he will have quite enough to do without that.

LINGER LONG* *Four to six players*

As you will guess from its name the winner of this game is the player who can keep his cards for the longest time.

You need an ordinary pack of cards.

The dealer is chosen by drawing as described on p. 14. After the player on his right has shuffled he gives out the cards, one at a time, face down to each player, going round to his left. If four people are playing he gives each of them nine cards; five people each get eight cards; while six people get seven each.

The last card which the dealer gives to himself, that is the last card dealt, is turned face up and shown to all the other players. Cards of the same suit as this card are trumps for the game.

The remaining cards are put together in a pile, face down, in the middle of the table.

When the cards have all been given out each player picks up his own cards and looks at them.

The player on the dealer's left chooses a card from his hand and puts it face up in the middle of the table. Each player in turn, going round to the left, must then play a card of the same suit if he has one. If he does not have a card of the same suit he can either play a card from the trump suit, or throw away a card from one of the other two suits.

A trump beats any other card except a higher trump – the 2 of trumps beats any ace except the ace of trumps and any other trump beats the 2 of trumps.

After all the players have put out one card, the player who has put out the highest card of the suit led has won the trick, unless it has been trumped, when the player who put out the highest trump will have won. The cards in the trick are then turned over and put on one side.

The winner of the trick takes the top card off the pile in the middle of the table and puts it in his hand. He then chooses one of his cards, which can be the one he has just picked up or any other, and puts it face up in the middle of the table as the first card of the next trick. Play goes round as before to the left.

As soon as a player has run out of cards he stops playing but the others carry on.

The winner is the player who manages to carry on longest, and still has one or more cards when everybody else has none.

You will see that it is best to take as many tricks as you can because that is the only way you can get more cards into your hand. You must watch which cards the other players put out very carefully and see if you can guess which cards they have left.

STAY AWAY* *Four players*

In this intriguing game for four players you do not try to take the tricks yourself but try to make the other players take them.

The object of the game is not to take any tricks with jacks in them. If you take the jack of spades in a trick, you lose three points, but the other three jacks count only one point each.

It is best for four players but five or six can play. Just as for *Rolling Stone* you arrange the pack so that when it is all dealt each player will have eight cards. For four players you use the 7s, 8s, 9s, 10s, jacks, queens, kings and aces. For five players you add the 5s and 6s and for six players you only throw out the 2s.

If six people are playing it is probably best to use the 9s as the cards to avoid rather than the jacks.

The dealer is chosen by drawing as described on p. 14. After the player on his right has shuffled he gives out the cards one at a time, face down, to each player, going round the table to his left until all the cards have been given out.

Each player then picks up his cards and looks at them. The player on the dealer's left chooses a card and puts it face up in the middle of the table. The player on his left must play a card of the same suit if he can, but if he does not have one he can throw away a card from one of the other three suits (a good way to get rid of a jack).

If a player does not follow suit even though he has got a card of that suit he loses a point.

When all the players have put out one card, the player who has put out the highest card of the suit led has won the trick and gathers the cards together from the centre of the table. He puts the trick in front of him as a neat face-down pile.

He then chooses a card from his hand and puts it face up in the middle of the table as the first card of the next trick. Play goes on as before to the left.

When all the cards have been played each player turns up the tricks he has won and the scores are marked down – three points to the player who has won the jack of spades, and one point to the players who have won the other jacks. Of course, if you win all four jacks you are given six points.

As soon as any player has ten points the game stops. The winner is the player with fewest points, but, if two players have the same smallest number of points, you can play once more adding up the points they score in this game to see who is the winner.

THIRTY-ONE* *Three or more players (the more the better)*

A simple game in which you have to be able to add up quickly if you are going to win.

You need an ordinary pack of cards.

The object of the game is to collect three cards of the same suit which add up to thirty-one, or to get three cards of the same value.

Aces count eleven, kings, queens, jacks and 10s count ten each, and the other cards count according to the number of pips on them. The only way to get three cards which add up to thirty-one is to collect an ace and two cards worth ten each, for example the ace, queen and jack of clubs.

Three cards of the same value count as thirty-and-a-half points and beat everything else except three cards of one suit which add up to thirty-one. Three aces will beat three kings, and so on down to three 2s which are the lowest three-of-a-kind.

The dealer is chosen by drawing as described on p. 14 and the player on his right shuffles the cards. The dealer then gives out three cards to each player, one at a time, face down, going round to the left, and also deals three cards face up in the middle of the table.

Each player picks up the cards in front of him and looks at them.

The player on the dealer's left exchanges any one of his cards with one of those face up on the table. The player on his left then exchanges one of his cards for one of the three face-up cards on the table and so on round to the left.

The game goes on like this until one player thinks he has three cards in his hand which will beat any other hand that will be shown. When it is his turn to exchange cards he does not do so but knocks on the table to show he is 'content'. All the other players now have to change cards once, in turn, until the turn comes back to the player who knocked.

Each player then shows his hand and the player with the best hand wins.

You do not have to wait until you have a thirty-one or three-of-a-kind before you knock. Sometimes it is better to be 'content' with a fair hand (one that adds up to twenty-nine or thirty, for example) so that you can stop the other players from getting better hands by exchanging cards. A hand that adds up to thirty beats any other hand that adds up to less.

You can either keep a score sheet showing the number of rounds each player has won or you can play the game for counters.

GUESS IT*   *Two players*

This simple bluffing game was invented by Rufus Isaacs who is an American expert on games of all kinds.

To play it you need one complete suit from an ordinary pack of cards.

The dealer is chosen by one player shuffling the cards and dealing them out, one at a time, face up, first to his opponent and then to himself. The player who gets the ace is the dealer for the first game.

The non-dealer shuffles the cards and cuts them by taking the top half of the pack and putting it on the table, taking care that no one can see the bottom card of this half. The bottom half of the pack is then put on top of this part.

The top card is dealt face down into the middle of the table and the remaining cards are given out, one at a time, face down, to each player until none are left.

The players pick up their cards and look at them.

The object of the game is to guess the value of the face-down card.

The non-dealer asks the dealer if he has a particular card – for example, 'Do you have the 7?' He can ask for a card that is in his hand or for one that is not. The dealer must answer truthfully.

No card can be asked about twice.

The dealer, in his turn, asks if the other player has a card and gets a truthful answer. They continue asking in turn until one player thinks that he knows the value of the face-down card.

When it is his turn the player can say what he thinks the face-down card is. The card is turned over and if the player is right he has won. If he is wrong he has lost.

Suppose Margaret and Francis are playing and that Margaret dealt. She has Q–J–9–7–3–2 and Francis has A–K–10–8–5–4.

Francis asks first and says, 'Have you the jack?'

Margaret says 'Yes' and puts the jack face up on the table. She then asks 'Have you the 2?'

Francis says 'No' and thinks like this: 'Either she has the 2 or not. If she has the 2, she is bluffing and I needn't bother.

'If she doesn't have the 2, and I do not guess that the face-down card is the 2, she will name it correctly on her next turn.' He decides she is bluffing and asks 'Do you have the 6?'

Margaret says 'No'. Because she was bluffing on her last turn, and because Francis will be able to work out that she has the 2, she puts it, face up, on the table before asking her next question. She thinks much as Francis did: 'Either he has the 6 or not and if I don't guess correctly this time he will do it next.'

She decides he is not bluffing, says, 'It is the 6', turns up the card and finds she has won.

FROGS IN THE POND*   *Two to six players (best for four)*

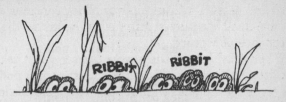

This game needs a lot of concentration because if you do not watch out for and remember the high cards you will almost certainly lose.

As well as giving cards to each player in this game you also deal out cards to a separate pile. These cards are the 'frogs'.

Before you start you have to arrange the pack so that when all the cards are given out all the players and the 'frog' pile will get the same number. If three people are going to play you do not have to do anything (since the fifty-two cards will deal out as thirteen for each player and thirteen 'frogs'). For two players you take a 2 away – usually the 2 of clubs; for four players you take two 2s away; for five players you take all four 2s but for six players you only take three 2s.

The dealer is chosen by drawing as described on p. 14. After the player on his right has shuffled the pack, the dealer gives out the cards one at a time, face down, to each player but also putting one card face down in the middle of the table after each round.

When all the cards have been given out the players pick up their own cards and look at them. The pile in the middle of the table is only put together tidily at this point. No one looks at any of the cards in it.

The object of the game is to score 100 points before

anyone else does so. You score points by winning certain cards in tricks.

Each: 10 counts ten   points
     5 counts five   points
     ace counts four   points
     king counts three   points
     queen counts two   points
     jack counts one   point

If you add up all these scores you will find that 100 points must be won in each round of the game.

The player on the dealer's left chooses a card from his hand and places it face up in the middle of the table. The player on his left must play a card of the same suit if he can. If he does not have a card of the same suit he must throw away one of his other cards. If he makes a mistake and throws away a card when he could have followed suit, he loses ten points.

When all the players have put out one card, the player who played the highest card in the suit first led wins the trick. He gathers up the cards from the middle of the table and puts them as a neat pile in front of him. He also takes the top card from the pile of 'frogs' and puts it on top of the trick he has just won. He can look at the frog but must be very careful not to let anyone else see what it is. He then puts out the first card for the next trick, face up in the middle of the table.

The winner of each trick takes the next frog, looks at it if he likes, and puts it with the trick he has just taken. It is never put among the cards in his hand.

When all the cards have been played, and all the frogs have been taken, each player turns over the tricks he has taken and counts up the number of points he has made. These scores are written down, the cards are shuffled, and are dealt out by the player on the left of the last dealer.

The first player to score 100 points is the winner.

The game can also be played with partners, two against two, but remember that the same rule about the frogs still holds – you must not let anyone else see your frog, not even your partner.

Sometimes the game is played with a 'Tadpole'. This is usually the jack of spades and the player who wins the Tadpole loses ten points when the scores are added up.

BOHEMIAN SCHNEIDER*   *Two players*

This version of a German game has a method of taking tricks which is unique. It is not exactly the same as the game which was originally described to me but I feel it is more interesting.

The object of the game is to collect as many points in scoring cards as possible – 10s count 10, jacks 2, queens 3, kings 4, aces 11 and the rest nothing. This means that the total number of points in the pack is 120.

Two people play the game and use the thirty-two-card piquet pack (all the cards from the 7s to the aces).

One person is chosen as dealer as described on p. 14, and he shuffles the cards and deals six cards to each player, three at a time, face down. The remaining cards are placed face down in the centre of the table as a stock.

The non-dealer chooses a card from his hand and places it face up in the middle of the table. His opponent can only beat the card led by playing a card one higher in face value – suits do not count. In order of face value, the seven is lowest, and then come the 8, 9, 10, jack, queen, king and ace, the ace being the highest.

Suppose Rosemary leads a 10. Veronica could beat this with a jack (and know she had won 12 points). If Veronica plays any other card, Rosemary will take them both (and count their point value to her score).

In *Bohemian Schneider* you do not have to follow suit and there are no trumps.

The winner of each trick takes the top card from the stock and puts it in his hand; the loser takes the second card. The winner of one trick also leads to the next.

When all the stock has been taken, play continues until all the cards have been played.

The players then count up how many points they have won in scoring cards. The winner is the player with most points. A score of from 61 to 90 counts as a single game; 91 to 119 is a double game, while 120 is a triple game. After a tie, with each player getting exactly 60 points, the value of the next game is increased by one level (so that a single game becomes a double; a double becomes a triple, and so on).

In *Bohemian Schneider* you have to be very careful about which cards you lead. Leading a 9 is often bad because your opponent can win it with a 10 and score 10 points. Leading a jack is bad, because your opponent can save a 10. In fact something can be said against leading any of the cards except the 7s and 8s – and they are valuable for throwing away. It is this constant choice between bad and worse which makes the game interesting.

GERMAN WHIST*   *Two players*

A good game for two players, *German Whist* depends on paying attention to the cards that have been played so that you can work out which cards your opponent has left.

An ordinary pack of fifty-two cards is used.

The dealer is chosen by drawing as described on p. 14 and the other player shuffles the cards.

The dealer gives out thirteen cards each to himself and his opponent, one at a time, face down, with the first card being given to his opponent.

The card on top of the pile, the twenty-seventh, is

turned face up and placed on the table next to the pile, which is put face down.

All cards of the same suit as the face-up card count as trumps for that round. A trump card beats all other cards except a higher trump – the 2 of trumps beats all other cards except any trumps, and is beaten by all other trumps.

Aces are high in *German Whist*.

The players pick up the cards in front of them and look at them.

The player who did not deal chooses a card from his hand and places it face up on the table. The dealer must play a card of the same suit if he can. If it is a higher card he will win the trick; if it is a lower card he will lose.

If the dealer does not have any cards of the suit led he can win by playing a trump or lose by throwing away one of the cards in the other two suits.

The winner of the trick takes the face-up card from beside the pile and adds it to the other cards in his hand. The loser of the trick picks up the top card from the (face-down) pile and adds it to the cards in his hand. Of course, he does not let his opponent see what it is.

The next card of the pile is then turned up and placed on the table next to the pile. Trumps do not change even if this card is not of the same suit as the first one.

The winner of the trick then chooses a card from his hand and places it face up on the table as the first card of the next trick.

The game goes on in this way until the pile has been completely used up.

All the tricks that have been taken in the game up to this point are gathered together and put to one side, as a face-down pile.

The players then play for the last thirteen tricks. The winner of the last face-up card leads the first card in this part of the game and the winner of each trick after that leads to the next trick.

Trumps stay exactly as they were at the beginning.

The winner of the game is the player who gets most tricks out of the last thirteen.

As a change you may like to play so that the winner is the player who takes fewer tricks out of the last thirteen. You must still keep a trump suit and will find that you must change the whole way you approach the game.

HEARTS* *Two to six players (best with four)*

This is an easy game for young players but it needs just enough skill to interest the older ones.

If four people are playing they can play as partners but for any other number it is probably best for each person to play for himself.

The object of the game is not to win any hearts.

You use an ordinary fifty-two-card pack but for three players you must take out a black 2. For five players you take out both black 2s, while for six players you take out all four 2s.

If two people are going to play it is best to follow the rules for *German Whist*, but to count the hearts in all the tricks.

The game described here is for three to six players.

The dealer is chosen by drawing as described on p. 14 and the player on his right shuffles the pack.

The dealer gives out all the cards, one at a time, to each player, face down, going round to the left.

The players pick up the cards in front of them and look at them.

The player on the dealer's left chooses any card from his hand and puts it face up in the middle of the table. Then, each player in turn, going round to the left, either puts out a card of the same suit or, if he does not have any, throws away one of his other cards. It is a good idea to throw away high hearts if you can.

Ace beats king, king beats queen and so on down to the 2.

When all the players have put out a card, the player who played the highest card in the suit first led wins the trick and puts all the cards in it face down on the table in front of him in a neat pile.

He then puts out the first card of the next trick and play goes round to the left as before.

This continues until the players have used up all their cards. They then turn over the tricks they have taken and each player counts the number of hearts he has won.

The player who has the fewest hearts is the winner. If two or more players have the same lowest number of hearts then a new game is played and the score for it is added on to the score for the first game, to find who has the smallest number.

If two people want to play *Hearts* it is probably best for the dealer to give out thirteen cards to each, one at a time. The rest of the pack is placed face down in the middle of the table and the top card is turned over.

The player who did not deal puts out the first card from his hand and the dealer follows suit if he can.

The winner of the trick takes the face-up card and the loser takes the face-down card off the top of the pile. The winner also leads the first card for the next trick after the new top card has been turned over.

This goes on until all the cards have been taken from the stock pile. The last thirteen tricks are then played for and the winner is the player who has taken fewest hearts in all the tricks.

There are so many variations of *Hearts* that it is impossible to describe them all here.

A good variation is to let each heart count for its pip value, with ace counting fourteen points, king thirteen, queen twelve, and jack eleven. In this game you have to watch very carefully which hearts you are being given by your opponents. It is also a good idea to play this form of the game for a set number of times – say, five or ten. The scores are written down at the end of each round and are added up at the end. The winner is the player with the smallest number of points.

Sometimes another card, like the queen of spades, is taken as being worth thirteen hearts against the player who takes it. These games have names like *Black Lady* or *Red Jack Hearts* depending on the colour of the penalty card.

GOPS* *Two players*

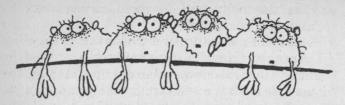

Gops is a fascinating game that can easily be played in an odd five or ten minutes. But you can play it over and over again without getting bored and you will always find new ways to play.

It is not like most other card games since there is little luck in it. The winner is usually the player who has the most skill.

One other interesting thing about *Gops* is that you always know which cards your opponent has in his hand. Even so, he may bluff you into thinking he has put out a high card when it is really a low one.

To play the game you first sort a pack of cards into suits (hearts, clubs, diamonds and spades) and give one player all thirteen clubs, while the other player takes all thirteen spades. The thirteen diamonds are shuffled and placed in a pile face down on the table, taking care that no one sees the order they are in.

The hearts are not used.

In *Gops* you try to win as many points in diamonds as possible. The ace is worth one point, the 2 is worth two points and so on for all the cards with pips. The jack is worth eleven points, the queen twelve points and the king thirteen points. Remember, you are not trying to end up with the larger number of cards but the larger number of points, so that it is better to win the 10 than the 2.

In playing for the diamonds, the clubs and spades go

in the usual order with the ace being the smallest card and the king the highest – a queen beating a jack, for example and 9 beating 3.

To start the game, turn over the top card of the pile of diamonds and place it face up on the table.

Each player then chooses one card from his hand and places it face *down* on the table, taking care that the other player does not see what it is. When both players have done this, they turn over the cards they have chosen and show them to each other. The player who has chosen the higher card takes the diamond which is face up and puts it, still face up, on his right.

The other player does not take any card.

Each player then puts the club or spade that he has used on his left. All the cards that have been used stay face up on the table so that both players can see them all the time. But they cannot be used more than once.

The next diamond is then turned over and, as before, each player chooses one card from his hand and puts it face down on the table. They then turn them over at the same time. Again the player who has chosen the higher card takes the face-up diamond and puts it, face up, on his right.

If at any time the players choose cards of equal value, the next diamond is turned over and is placed beside the diamond that is already face up on the table. The players then choose cards from their hands as before but the winner in this case takes both the face-up cards.

If the result is still a draw, the next diamond is added to the other two and the players try to win all three. And so on until one player wins all the cards that are face up.

When all the diamonds have been won (and that means that neither player has any cards left in his hand, as well) the players add up the values of the diamond cards that they have on their right (remember that the ace is one point, the 2 is two points, and so on, and that the jack is eleven points, the queen is twelve points and the king is thirteen points). The player who has the bigger total is the winner.

At first sight, and maybe when you first play *Gops*, you will not see the point of the game. One quickly learns that, because the cards each have a different value, it is not a good idea to win the ace of diamonds with a king. If you do put out a king for the ace of diamonds, your opponent will know that you do not have any cards bigger than the queen and that you cannot beat his king.

Sometimes it pays to put out a low card when the face-up card is the king of diamonds or the queen. If your opponent thinks you have put out a high card, he will put out a high card to beat you (or to draw with you). By putting out a little card, you have made him waste a big one. This means that you will be able to beat all the cards he holds with the big ones you have saved and will, later on, win several cards which are, together, worth more than the king or queen you let him win.

The chances of bluffing one's opponent are very great in *Gops* and you can sometimes make him think you have put out a high card when it is really a low one. And sometimes make him think you have put out a low one when it is really a high one. As with all bluffing games it is important to alter the way in which you play. If you always bluff in the same way, your opponent will quickly see what you are doing and be able to beat you.

Before you start bluffing always look at the cards your opponent has played. You will then be able to work out which cards he has left in his hand. When you have done this, look at the cards in your hand. Then try to work out what he will play and what you should play to beat him. But remember that he is doing the same thing about you.

DUDAK** *Four players*

My old friend Mihail Arnautov showed me this variation of a simple German children's game. It is best for
four players and this is the version I will describe, but it
should be obvious how to change the rules for two or
three.

The object of the game is to get rid of all the cards from
your hand but the game continues until all the players
except one have got rid of their cards. The last player
holding cards is the loser. This is not a game you win, it
is one you lose.

The game is played with the thirty-two-card piquet
pack (all the cards from the 7s to the aces). The cards
rank in value from the aces down to the 7s in the normal
order.

The first dealer is chosen as described on p. 14. He
shuffles the cards, has them cut by the player on his
right and deals them all, one at a time, face down, to the
players.

The player on the dealer's left chooses any card he
likes from his hand and places it face up in the middle of
the table.

During the course of the game a pile of face-up cards
grows in the middle of the table. It is called a pile even if
it only has one card in it.

Each player, in his turn, can take as many cards as he

likes from the pile and put them in his hand. If a player takes the last card of the pile, his turn ends and the next player puts out any card he chooses to start a new pile.

So long as there are cards left in the pile, a player must put out a card which beats the top card. He can do this either by playing a card in the same suit (but higher in value) or by naming his own trumps and playing one of them. Of course, his trump suit must be different from the top card if he wants to play a card of lower value. He can name the suit of the top card so long as he plays a higher value card in the same suit.

Once a player has named his trump suit he cannot change it during the hand.

After beating the top card of the pile, the player adds to it any card he chooses from his hand and his turn ends.

If a player beats the top card of the pile with the last card from his hand, the pile is 'dead'. It is put aside and no cards can be taken from it. The next player starts a new pile with any card from his hand.

A player with no cards in his hand is 'out' and takes no further part in the play of the hand.

The loser is the last player left holding cards.

Because each player has his own personal trump suit, *Dudak* presents many interesting problems. If Francis has clubs for trumps and plays the ace, it can be beaten by Rosemary's 2 of diamonds if that is her trump suit.

The difficulty of the game can be increased by playing *Secret Dudak*. In this version, each player chooses one card from his hand at the beginning and places it, face down, in front of him. When it is his turn to play he can, if he wishes, turn this card over. His personal trump suit becomes that of the revealed card, which he must play immediately.

RUMMY** *Two to six players (four, five or six best)*

Rummy is an excellent family game which is very easily learnt and provides constant interest. The game is played very widely and has many different sets of rules. I shall describe a simple set which will allow you to play the game with enjoyment. But, if you want to play with a stranger, agree on which rules you are going to play before you start.

You need an ordinary pack of fifty-two cards.

The dealer having been chosen by drawing, as described on p. 14, the player on his right shuffles. The dealer then gives out the cards one at a time, face down, going round to the left.

If two people are playing, each one gets ten cards; if three are playing, they each get seven cards; with four or more players, they each get six cards.

Once all the cards have been given out the remainder of the pack is put, face down, on the table and the top card of the pile is turned over and placed beside it.

The object of the game is to get rid of all the cards in your hand by collecting certain patterns which you can put on the table.

The patterns are:

1. *Threes* – three cards of the same value, like three 5s, or three kings.

2. *Fours* – four cards of the same value, like four 2s or four kings.

3. *Sequence* – three, or more, cards of the same suit arranged in order of value. For example, 7–8–9 of clubs, or 9–10–J of diamonds. Aces are always low so that A–2–3 of hearts is a sequence but Q–K–A of spades is not. K–A–2 is never a sequence. The sequence can be of any length you like as long as the cards are in order – A–2–3–4–5–6–7–8 of diamonds is a sequence.

A card is either in a sequence or in a three or four – it cannot be in both at the same time.

When the cards have been given out the players pick them up and look at them. The player on the dealer's left either takes the face-up card or the top card from the pile (of course, he does not let anyone else see the value of this card) and puts it into his hand. He must then throw away a card from his hand (it could be the card he has just picked off the top of the pile). He puts this 'discard' beside the pile, either replacing the face-up card or covering it.

The next player, in his turn, can choose between the top card of the face-up pile and the top card of the face-down one. He discards a card and the turn passes to his left and so on round the table.

You get rid of one set of cards in your hand (which make a Three, a Four or a Sequence) after you have taken a card from the middle but before you have discarded. You can get rid of only one set at each turn.

After you have taken a card from the middle, you can join *one* card on to any sets which have already been put out by other players. For example, suppose a player has put out the 8–9–10 of diamonds and you hold the 7 and jack of that suit. You can play either one of these cards on to his sequence when it is your turn, and the other on the next round. You must always discard a card on to the pile in the middle after putting out a card in this way. The next player then has his turn.

The first player to get rid of all his cards is the winner and scores points for all the cards held by the other players. Aces count one, 2s two, and so on up to jacks, which count eleven, queens twelve, and kings thirteen.

If the face-down pile is used up before anyone has gone out, the face-up pile is shuffled and put face down in the middle of the table. The top card is turned over and is treated as the top card of a new face-up pile.

Suppose Margaret, Veronica, Francis and Rosemary are playing *Rummy* and that Rosemary deals:

Margaret	K♡, K◇, 6◇, 6♣, 2♣, A♡
Veronica	5♡, 5♠, 5♣, J♣, 8♣, A◇
Francis	3♠, 2◇, Q♣, 9♡, 7♣, 6♠
Rosemary	A♣, A♠, 9♣, 9◇, 10♡, 8♠

The first face-up card is the 6♡.

Margaret is the first to play and can make three 6s by taking the face-up card. She does this, puts her three 6s on the table (face up) and puts out the 2♣ as the new face-up card.

Veronica lifts the top card of the face-down pile – it is the Q♡. She puts out her three 5s and discards the Q♡ on top of the 2♣.

Francis decides to take the top card of the face-down pile – it is the 8◇. He puts the 6♠ on Margaret's 6s and discards the Q♣.

Rosemary also takes the top card of the face-down pile – the 9♣. She puts out her three 9s and discards the 10♡.

Margaret takes the top card – the 2♠ – and discards it. Veronica draws the K♣ and discards it. Francis draws the 3♣, puts the 9♡ on Rosemary's 9s and discards the 8◇.

Rosemary draws the 4◇ and discards the 8♠. Margaret draws the 5◇, puts it on Veronica's 5s and discards the K◇ because she has seen a king thrown away and realizes she will probably not be able to collect three kings. Veronica draws the J♡ and discards the 8♣ because she has seen two 8s thrown away. Francis draws the 3♡, puts out his three 3s, and discards the 7♣.

Play goes on in this way until one player manages to play out all his cards and discard the last on to the face-up pile.

Some people play *Rummy* with a joker. This is a special card which is allowed to count for any card, and the person holding it can choose whichever value he wants for it – in 9♡–joker–J♡ the joker counts as the 10♡, in A◇–joker–A♠–A♣ the joker counts as the A♡.

Once a combination has been put down including the joker, any player can, on his turn and after he has drawn a card, exchange the joker for the card it represents, if he has that card in his hand.

Another way of playing is to count all 2s as jokers which can represent any other card.

GIN RUMMY**   *Two players*

In this version of *Rummy* you need rather more skill and must watch the discard pile carefully so that you can work out what your opponent is trying to collect.

You need an ordinary pack of fifty-two cards.

First choose the dealer by drawing – the loser shuffles the cards. The dealer then gives each player ten cards, one at a time, face down, with the first card going to his opponent.

The twenty-first card is turned face up and put on the table beside the remainder of the pack (which is face down).

As in ordinary *Rummy* you are trying to get rid of the cards from your hand by making Threes, Fours and Sequences.

The non-dealer takes either the face-up card or the top card of the face-down pile into his hand, and discards one card on to the face-up pile. He can discard the card he has just drawn if he wants to.

The dealer, in his turn, takes either the face-up card or the top face-down one and discards.

The play goes on like this until one player decides to 'go down' by putting all his cards face up on the table. You can go down only when the point count in your hand is ten or less. Any Threes, Fours or Sequences do not count so they are put on the table. The point count is the total number of pips in the cards left in your hand once you have sorted out the Threes, Fours and Sequences. Aces count one, 2s two, and so on up to jacks, queens and kings, which each count ten.

You go down after you have drawn a card but before you discard. You must, however, discard one card on to the face-up pile after you have put cards on to the table – you cannot go down with eleven cards.

As soon as one of the players has gone down, his opponent puts his cards face-up on the table. He sorts out any Threes, Fours, and Sequences since they do not count, and adds any cards he can to his opponent's Threes and Sequences. Only then does he add up the pip value of his hand.

The player with the lower point score is the winner.

If the player who went down first is the winner, he scores the difference between the two counts.

If the player who went down first loses, his opponent scores the difference between the two counts *plus* ten points for 'under-cut'.

For example, if Margaret goes down first for a point count of five and Veronica goes down for nineteen, Margaret scores fourteen (19 − 5). But if Margaret goes down first for nine points and Veronica then goes down for two, Veronica scores seventeen points (9 − 2 + 10).

If a player goes down with all his cards (leaving none in his hand and giving a point count of zero), he scores a 'gin' and gets twenty points as well as the number of points in his opponent's hand. (If the other player also puts out all his cards, the first player still gets twenty points.)

The scores are written down. The last dealer shuffles the cards, and the non-dealer becomes the new dealer for the next round.

The game continues until one player reaches 100 points.

Suppose that Margaret and Veronica play *Gin Rummy* with Veronica dealing.

Margaret has the J–Q–K♢, J♣, K♡, 8–9♡, 5♢, 5♣, A♣.

Veronica has the 9♠, 9♢, 9–8–7♣, 7♡, 5♠, 5♡, 4♠, A♠.

The face-up card is the 10♣.

Margaret takes the 10♣, discards the A♣.

Veronica takes the A♣, discards the 4♠.

Margaret draws the A♢, discards the A♢.

Veronica takes the A♢, discards the 5♠.

Margaret takes the 5♠, discards the 9♡.

Veronica takes the 9♡, discards the 7♡.

(Although Veronica has a point count of only five, she decides to try one more draw.)

Margaret draws the 2♡, discards the 8♡.

Veronica draws the 2♢ and goes down.

She puts the 9♡, 9♠, 9♢, the 7–8–9♣ and the A♠, A♣, A♢ to one side, leaving her with the 2♢ and the 5♡. She discards the 5♡ and her point count is, therefore, two.

Margaret then has to go down. She puts the 5♢, 5♣, 5♠ and J–Q–K♢ to one side, adds the 10 and J♣ to Veronica's sequence and is left with the 2♡ and the K♡, a score of twelve.

Veronica's score is $12 - 2 = 10$.

Margaret deals to the next hand.

CRIBBAGE** *Two to four players*

Cribbage has a peculiar excitement all of its own. To play it well you have to be ready to seize any opportunity you can of scoring but, at the same time, you must also stop your opponent scoring. The game is never dull, something is always happening, and the lead can change hands many times before the end is reached.

The game was invented over three hundred years ago by Sir John Suckling, who is supposed to have won over twenty thousand pounds by sending out marked cards to all the gambling houses in the country. The game still has a very 'English' character and its rules are very nearly the same all over the world.

Cribbage can be played by two, three or four people and is equally good for all these numbers. There are three forms of the game – five-card, six-card and seven-card cribbage. I shall describe the six-card game for two players. All the other variations are described in most good books of card games. The description looks very long and complicated but, although there is a lot to remember, each little part is very simple and you will soon find that the game begins to make sense.

The object of all forms of *Cribbage* is to score points. Because of the speed with which points are scored, and the very large number of small scores that are made, it is difficult to keep the score by adding up on a piece of paper. Usually the score is kept on a cribbage board which, as can be seen in the diagram, is divided into two identical halves, each containing two rows of thirty holes collected together in fives, that is sixty holes in tens. At each end, in the centre of the board between the lines of holes, are the two *Game* holes. The best cribbage boards use ivory pegs but bone, wood or plastic ones are just as good, and used matches are very common. Each player needs two pegs.

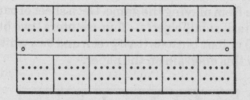

The cribbage board is put on the table between the two players but to one side. It should point acróss the table so that each player has one double row of holes near him. The hole at the left-hand end of the board is the Game hole for each player.

Scoring is done like this. At the beginning of the game the pegs are not stuck into the board. Suppose your first score is two. You must put a peg into the second hole of the row nearest to you, counting from the end where your Game hole is, that is the left-hand end. If your next score is three you put your second peg three holes in front of the first one, counting to the right. You keep counting in this way, always moving the peg from the back over the other one and putting it the correct number of holes ahead. When you reach the end of the outside line of holes you start counting back towards your Game hole on the inside line of holes.

In those games which are scored to sixty-one you go once round and the winner is the first player to be able to put a peg in his Game hole. You just need to have more than sixty points to do this, you do not have to count out exactly. If you have fifty-eight and get two points you have not won; if you have fifty-eight and get three points or more you can put your peg in the Game hole.

In those games which are scored to 121 you go twice round before putting a peg in the Game hole. If the race is to 181, you go three times round.

Not everyone has a cribbage board but this need not stop you from playing the game. Get a sheet of paper and two pairs of small objects – four counters (two blue and two red) or four buttons (two green and two white).

Draw this diagram on the paper:

6	8	L	9	S	captured	ε	Z	l
01		02		0ε	04		0S	09
•								•
60		50		40	30		20	10
1	2	3		4	5	6	7	8	9

and use it as your cribbage board. If you score five, put a counter on the 5 on your side of the board. When you score seven more (making twelve altogether) you put a counter on the 10 and move the first one on to the 2 (10 and 2 makes twelve). Of course you will have to be much

more careful about your adding-up with this board but it
will soon be very easy for you.

The dealer is chosen by choosing cards from the
spread-out pack – aces count low and the player with the
lower card is the dealer. The dealer shuffles the cards
and the other player cuts the pack. That is he takes
about half the cards off the top of the pack and puts them
down on the table without letting the dealer see the
bottom card. He then puts the remaining cards on top of
this part of the pack and the dealer can now deal.

Six-card Cribbage

The dealer gives each player six cards, one at a time,
face down.

Cribbage can be divided into several parts. Immediately after the deal each player has to put two cards
from his own hand into the dealer's 'crib' – a group of
cards on which the dealer scores points at the end of each
hand. Once the cards have been put in the crib, each
player shows his cards one at a time, trying to score
points for play. After the play is over, each player counts
the number of points scored in his hand with the non-
dealer scoring first. Then the dealer counts the number
of points in his crib and this is the end of the hand.

The non-dealer picks up all the cards and shuffles
them and is the dealer for the new hand.

Each time you score you must move your pegs on the
cribbage board. If you do not take a score as soon as you
have called it, you lose all chance of getting it.

When you have picked up your six cards and looked at
them, you must choose which two you are going to put
away. To help you decide you must work out how many
points you will score with the four cards that are left.
You will see how to do this below. You will also choose to

throw away different cards if you are dealer ('your crib') or if the other player is ('his crib'). Obviously if it is your crib you try to put cards in it which will help you to score while if it is his crib you will try to put cards in it which will be no use to him.

Once both players have put cards into the crib, the non-dealer cuts the pack by lifting off the top half. He is careful not to see the bottom card, nor to let the dealer see it. The dealer picks up the top card of the pile left on the table and turns it over so that both players can see it. He then puts it back, still face up, on top of the pack.

This card is very important and is called the *Start*. If it is a jack the dealer can take two *for his heels* as soon as the jack is turned up. If the two points are not scored before the dealer has played a card this score is lost.

Once the Start has been turned up, the players take it in turn to play cards out on to the table, one at a time face up. In doing this they try to score points either by making the total number of pips add up to certain numbers or by playing the cards in certain orders. Each player puts the cards face up in front of him since they will be used for *counting* later on.

The non-dealer chooses a card from his hand and lays it face up on the table in front of him, naming the number of pips it has at the same time. Kings, queens and jacks all count as ten pips as far as this is concerned but they keep their order (jack, queen, king) for other ways of scoring. The dealer then plays a card from his hand on to the table in front of him and names the sum of his card and the one already played. The non-dealer adds another card to his first one and names the sum of all three cards and so on, in turn. The sum must never go past thirty-one, however.

A player who can make the sum equal thirty-one scores two points.

A player who cannot make the sum equal thirty-one must play a card if he can, even if he thinks this will let the other player make the sum thirty-one.

A player who cannot put out any of the cards from his hand because they each make the sum pass thirty-one must say 'No' or knock on the table to show that he cannot go. The other player can then play out his cards, one at a time, naming the total sum after each card, until he reaches thirty-one or cannot play any of his cards because they would each make the sum pass thirty-one. If he makes the score come to thirty-one he gets two points. If he cannot play any more cards he must either say 'No' or knock on the table.

When both players have had to stop playing before thirty-one is reached the player who last put out a card scores one point, for *Go*.

As well as getting points for getting to thirty-one or Go the players can score points for making the cards from certain patterns or sums.

Fifteen – if the sum is exactly fifteen the player who put out the last card scores two points. For example if the non-dealer puts out a 9, saying 'Nine', the dealer can put out a 6, saying 'Fifteen', and scoring two points on the board as he says it.

Pairs – when a card is played which is of exactly the same value as the last card played, the player scores two points. Kings pair with kings, queens with queens, jacks with jacks and so on down.

Threes – when a third card of the same value as a Pair is played immediately after the Pair, the player scores six points.

Fours – when a fourth card of the same value as a Three is played immediately after the Three, the player scores twelve points.

Runs – three or more cards of any suits which can be

put into a regular order, like 5♣, 6♢, 7♠, 8♡. The cards do not have to be put down in order so long as they could be put in order. For example, 7♡, 5♣, 6♢ could be arranged in order 5–6–7 and would score as a Run. If the 8♡ is added next the four cards can be put into the order 5–6–7–8 and count as a new Run.

The player who puts out the last card of a Run scores one point for each card in it. A Run of three scores three points; of four, scores four points; of five, five points, and so on.

In all Runs the ace is low. This means A–2–3 is a Run, but Q–K–A is not.

Pairs, Threes, Fours and Runs can be scored by a player when he keeps on putting out cards after his opponent has knocked but the total sum must not pass thirty-one.

You can score in more than one of these arrangements at any one time. For example, your opponent puts out the 2♡. You put out the 7♢ (making nine) and he replies with the 3♣ (making twelve). If you put out the 3♡, you will score two points for the Fifteen and two more for the pair of 3s – four points altogether. If he plays the 8♣ (making twenty-three) and you can put out the 8♠ you will score two points for the Pair and two points for Thirty-one.

It is not a good idea to put out a card next in value to the last card played, or even a card that is two removed. This can let your opponent make a Run by filling in the middle or playing at one of the ends. For example, if he puts out a 9 and you put out a 10, he could score three points with either an 8 or a jack. Or, if he puts out a 9 and you put out a jack, he could score three points by putting out a 10.

Play does not stop when *Go* is scored since the non-scorer starts a new round with any card from his hand.

Play only stops, and counting starts, when both players have run out of cards.

The non-dealer starts *counting* by laying all his cards on the table in front of him, face up. The Start card on top of the pack also counts as part of his hand, so that if his four cards were J◇, 5♣, 4♡, 6◇ and the Start card was the 6♡ he counts all five cards as one hand.

The counting is done by looking for patterns among the cards and scoring points for them, just as in the play which has just finished. You move your peg at the end of your count.

Fifteens – any cards which add up to fifteen score two points. Thus a 10 and a 5 counts two, as do 9 and 6; 8 and 7; 10, 3 and 2; 9, 3, 2 and 1; 8, 4 and 3, and so on. Remember that kings, queens and jacks count as ten points so that queen and 5 is fifteen.

The same card can be counted in more than one Fifteen as long as the other cards are different. For example, if you have 10♠, 5♣, 5◇ you score 'Fifteen two' for the 10♠ + 5♣ and another 'Fifteen two' for the 10♠ + 5◇. You usually say 'Fifteen two', showing the first Fifteen, and 'Fifteen four' (that is, two plus two) when you show the second Fifteen. A 9–6–6 or an 8–7–7 also scores 'fifteen four'. With 9–6–6–6 you score 'fifteen six' (counting the 9 with each 6 in turn) and with 10–5–5–5 you score 'fifteen eight' (counting the 10 with each 5 in turn, and then counting all three 5s together). Four 5s also counts 'fifteen eight' because you can choose three 5s in four different ways.

Pairs – any two cards of the same value count as a Pair and score two points. Therefore Q–Q–6–6 counts 'four for pairs', while 9–9–6–6 scores 'fifteen eight and four for pairs, makes twelve'.

Threes – any three cards of the same value count as a Three and score six points. Therefore, 9–4–4–4 counts 'six for three 4s', while 8–7–7–7 scores 'fifteen six and six for three 7s, makes twelve'.

Scoring six for Threes is the same as counting two for Pairs, since you can make three different pairs with three cards.

Fours – any four cards of the same value count as a Four and score twelve. Therefore, 3–3–3–3 scores 'twelve for four 3s'. The only four that scores for Fifteens as well is 5–5–5–5. This scores 'fifteen eight, and twelve for four 5s, makes twenty'.

Runs – any three or more cards which can be arranged in order score one point for each card, a Run of three scoring three, one of four scoring four and so on. Moreover you can use the same cards in several different Runs. Suppose you have the 3♡, 4♢, 5♣, 5♠. You can arrange them as 3♡–4♢–5♣ (scoring three points) or as 3♡–4♢–5♠ (scoring another three points). If you hold 4♣–5♠–6♡–6♢, you score 'fifteen two (4♣, 5♠, 6♢), fifteen four (4♣, 5♠, 6♡), and two for a Pair (6♢, 6♡) makes six. Three for a Run (4♣, 5♠, 6♢) makes nine, and three for a Run (4♣, 5♠, 6♡) makes twelve.'

Flush – any four cards in the original hand (not counting the Start) which are of the same suit count as a Flush and score four. If the Start is also of the same suit you score five for a flush of five.

His Nob – you score one for *his nob* if your hand has the jack of the same suit as the Start.

When the non-dealer has finished his count, and has moved his peg on the cribbage board, the dealer puts his hand face up on the table and counts in the same way. The Start is taken to be part of his hand for this count.

After the dealer has counted his hand and has moved his peg he puts the four cards of his hand away and turns over the four cards in his crib (which were put aside at the beginning of the game) and counts it. The Start is taken to be part of his crib for this count. Suppose the crib is made up of 6◇, 7♡, 7♠ and 8◇, and the Start is the 8♣. You score 'Fifteen two (7♡, 8◇), fifteen four (7♡, 8♣), fifteen six (7♠, 8◇), fifteen eight (7♠, 8♣). Twelve for Runs (6◇, 7♡, 8◇; 6◇, 7♡, 8♣; 6◇, 7♠, 8◇; 6◇, 7♠, 8♣), making twenty. Two for a Pair (7♡, 7♠), making twenty-two, and two for another Pair (8◇, 8♣), making twenty-four.'

You can score a Flush in the crib only if all five cards are of the same suit. This counts as five points.

Once the dealer has pegged his score for the crib, the non-dealer picks up all the cards and shuffles them ready for the next hand.

The game continues until one player has won by managing to score more than 121 – he has been twice round the board and has put his peg in his Game hole before the other player has done so.

Cribbage is a game of skill and, to play it well, you must be able to choose the best cards to put in the crib and be able to score points in the play.

Choosing the cards for the crib can be difficult and even people who have played for a long time occasionally have to sit and think over the difficult choices they can make. Never worry about how long it takes you to make up your mind. At first, when you are learning to play *Cribbage*, it is all strange to you but after you have played it for a little time you will find that you can choose the cards for the crib as soon as you look at your hand.

The best way of dealing with this problem is to ask yourself first 'Is it my crib?' If it is your crib, you want to put cards in it that will score. If it is not your crib you want to put cards in it that will not score. It is a good idea, in some situations, to give up scoring points in your hand by putting scoring cards in your crib.

When you are getting near your Game hole you must watch the score carefully. It is the player who 'pegs out' first, gets his peg into the Game hole first, who wins. It does not matter if you would have had the higher score or not; if your opponent got to his Game hole before you got to yours he has won.

You will have realized that your decision on which cards to keep and which to throw away still depends on many things and I will now try to show the different ways you should look at a hand and deal with it.

Suppose you have been dealt Q♠–7♠–5♣–4♣–4♡–2♠.

If it is your crib you have no problems. You put the Q♠ and 5♣ into your crib (making sure of two points there, and maybe more) and keep 7♠, 4♣, 4♡, 2♠ in your hand, which gives a certain four points (*fifteen* two and two for a *Pair*). And these cards are quite good for counting as well.

But if it is your opponent's crib you have a problem. You do not want to give him the Q♠ and 5♣ – not only because of the score of two points but also to avoid the risk of him throwing either a 5 or a 10 into his crib, or a 10 turning up for the Start.

This means you must either keep 7♠, 5♣, 4♣, 2♠ (giving your opponent the Q♠ and 4♡) or the 5♣, 4♣, 4♡, 2♠ (giving him the Q♠, 7♠). The second of these is probably better since it scores two points anyway and has quite a good chance of being turned into a double Run (if either a 6 or a 3 is turned up for Start). It is also better for play.

However, if it is your opponent's crib, and you only need six points to peg out, you should look at the hand differently. Since it is your first count you need not worry about putting points into your opponent's crib. If you keep the 7♠, 4♣, 4♡, 2♠ you have four points in your hand and you should have a good chance of scoring two points in the play. It does not matter that you have put two points into his crib because you have a good chance of winning before he can count it.

Cribbage Patience

Whether you would like to practise your *Cribbage* or are looking for an interesting game to pass the time you cannot do much better than this form of *Patience*. All you need to know is how to play *Cribbage*.

You shuffle an ordinary pack of cards and deal out six cards to yourself and two to your crib. You can do this either by dealing three cards to yourself, two to the crib, and three to yourself, or two to yourself, one to the crib, two more to yourself, a second to the crib and the last two to yourself.

You pick up your six cards and put two into the crib.

The top card of the pack is then turned as for the Start.

There is no play in *Cribbage Patience*, you just count the score in your hand and then that in your crib, moving the pegs on the cribbage board as though you were playing a real opponent.

You put the eight used cards to one side, keep the Start as part of your new hand, deal out five more cards for your new hand and two for the new crib, and turn up another Start.

You will find that you can do this six times and that four cards will be left over. These are scored as a single crib, using the last Start to make the fifth card.

You will probably find it is difficult to score more than ninety.

2 DOMINO GAMES

The ordinary set of dominoes that you can buy in a toyshop has twenty-eight pieces in it. Each piece is a small rectangle of wood, bone or plastic that is made up of two squares. Each square has some dots on it (called pips by most players).

In the twenty-eight-domino set the squares can have any number of pips on them from none to six. You talk about each domino by stating the number of pips that is on each square.

The domino

is called the 'six-three' or the 'three-six'; the domino

is called the 'blank-three' or the 'three-blank'.

If the number of pips on each square is the same that domino is called a double. The domino

is called the 'double-five'; the domino

is called the 'double-one'.

The side of the domino with the pips on it is called its face; the other side is its back.

Some people call the twenty-eight-domino set the double-six set because the biggest double is the double-six.

Double-nine sets (with fifty-five pieces) can be bought in some shops and make for better games if there are going to be more than four players.

FOURS   *Two to five players*

This is a very simple game which young players enjoy. It does not need any real skill but it is a good way of learning how to play dominoes.

The dominoes are shuffled by mixing them face down on the table and each player turns over one domino. The player with the highest double is the dealer. If no double is turned over, the player whose domino has the most pips on it is the dealer.

The dominoes are all turned face down once more and the dealer shuffles them. He then gives out dominoes one at a time to all the players, going round to the left until there are not enough dominoes left to go right round. (There are no dominoes left over if two or four people are playing; there is one domino left if three people are playing; there are three dominoes left with five people.) Any spare dominoes are put to one side but are kept face down. They are not used in this game.

Each player picks up his dominoes and places them so that he can see the pips on them. Of course, he does not let anyone else see their faces.

The object of the game is to get rid of all your dominoes first.

The player sitting on the left of the dealer plays first. He chooses a domino from his hand and puts it, face up, in the middle of the table. He then looks at his hand to see if he has any other dominoes with the same number of pips as is on either end of the domino he has just played. If he has, he puts that domino face up on the table so that the matching ends touch one another. For example suppose he had the five-three and the three-two in his hand. If he puts out the five-three first he can then play the three-two.

He again looks at his dominoes to see whether he can match either of the ends of the chain (a five or a two in our example) and keeps on playing dominoes from his hand until he can no longer play a matching domino or until he gets rid of all his dominoes. If he can do this, he has won.

If a player has had to stop before he has got rid of all his dominoes the player on his left has a turn which lasts until he gets rid of all his dominoes (and wins) or cannot match the ends. It is then the turn of the player on his left and so on round the table until one player gets rid of all his dominoes.

It is possible to get rid of all your dominoes on the first turn. Suppose you have the double-six, six-five, six-two, five-three, four-one, three-blank, and two-one. You put out the double-six and match one of its ends with the six-two. You follow this with the two-one and four-one, leaving the six-five, five-three and three-blank in your hand. You put the six-five out next to the free end of the double-six and follow this with the five-three and the three-blank, getting rid of all your dominoes before anyone else has a turn, and winning the game. This only happens very rarely, however, and you usually find that each person has two turns before anyone gets rid of all their dominoes.

If it is found that no one can match either end each player adds up the number of pips on the dominoes he has left. The winner is the player with the smallest total in this case.

ENDS *Four players*

This is a very simple game for four people but it has a fascination of its own.

The dominoes are shuffled face down and each player takes seven.

The player with the double-six puts it face up in the middle of the table.

Each player in turn matches one of the ends of the chain with one of his own dominoes.

If, at any time, a player cannot go he must ask the player on his left to give him a suitable domino. If he gets one, he plays it and the player on his left then has his turn as usual.

If the player on his left does not have a suitable domino, he must ask the player on *his* left. If he gets a domino he gives it to the player who first asked and then takes his turn as usual. If he does not get a domino, the player he has asked must ask the player on *his* left. If he gets a suitable domino it is passed back to the first player and the second and third players take their turns as usual.

If the question is passed right round the table to the player who asked it first, he can then play any domino he likes.

The winner is the first player to get rid of all his dominoes.

One of the most interesting points about this game is that you can often choose the domino which you pass to the player on your right. This lets you, in effect, play two dominoes at once and this can be a great advantage.

DOMINO PATIENCE   *One player*

This is a splendid game for one and will teach you how to choose which domino to play in most domino games.

Shuffle the dominoes face down.

Choose five dominoes and look at them. Play one into the middle of the table and try to join as many of the others as possible on to the chain, matching ends as in the *Block Game*. When you have played as many as you can, take new dominoes from the boneyard until you again have five dominoes in your hand.

Once more, play as many as you can on to the chain.

Keep on doing this until you have played all the dominoes, or cannot go.

You have won the game if you manage to empty the boneyard completely.

You can make the game easier by taking six, or seven, dominoes in your hand at the beginning and taking dominoes from the boneyard to keep this number constant.

You do not have to play at matching ends. You could make the joining ends add up to seven, as in *Matador*, or you could play *Fives and Threes*, and try to score as many points as possible.

THE BLOCK GAME   *Two to four players*

There are very many ways of playing this game but most of them only change the rules very slightly. The rules for the game which I am going to describe have been chosen because this is a popular way of playing the *Block Game*. At the end I describe some of the changes that can be made to the rules and, if you already know a different way of playing this game, you may find that your way is written about there.

To choose who plays first you shuffle the dominoes face down on the table and then each player turns over one domino. The player with the highest double will play first, the player on his left next, and so on round the table. If no double is turned over, the player whose domino has the most pips on it plays first. Or you can choose again and wait until a double is turned over.

The dominoes are all turned face down once more and are shuffled again. Each player then chooses seven dominoes and places them so that he can see what they are. Of course, he does not let anyone else see their faces.

The object of the game is to get rid of all your dominoes.

Any dominoes which are not taken by the players (this will only happen when there are two or three players; four players take all the dominoes) are put on one side, still face down. Some players call these dominoes 'the stock', others call them the 'woodpile' or the 'boneyard'. This last name comes from the days when dominoes were made of bone, with the best ones being made of ivory.

The first player puts one of his dominoes, face up, in the middle of the table. The player on his left then looks at his dominoes to see if the number of pips on any of his dominoes is the same as that on either end of the domino in the middle. If one of his dominoes does match an end, he places that domino face up on the table so that the matching ends touch each other.

Suppose the first player put out the four-two.

The next player could put down any domino from his hand with a two on it, or a four.

Suppose he chooses the six-two (or the two-six).

The next player has to put down a domino that matches one of the ends of the chain (that is, a four or a six in the example). And so on round the table.

If a player cannot match either end of the chain with a domino in his hand, he must take one domino from the boneyard. He can put his domino in the middle if it matches one of the ends of the chain, but if it does not match he just keeps it and the next player has a turn. Of course, if there are no dominoes left in the boneyard, a player who cannot go loses his turn.

The first person to get rid of all his dominoes is the winner.

If it happens that no one can play and that the boneyard has been used up, then each player adds up the pips on all the dominoes he holds in his hand. The one who has the smallest total is the winner in this case.

In playing dominoes it is generally important to play the dominoes of which you have most in your hand. If you have four 'threes' and two 'sixes', it is better to play a three. Skill in playing dominoes comes from knowing when to block – that is, stop the other players from being able to play from their hands and make them take dominoes from the boneyard or miss a turn. To do this properly you have to be able to choose sensibly when you have several dominoes that you can play.

Remember that there are seven dominoes of each kind (these are sometimes called suits). There are seven blanks, and seven sixes; seven ones and seven fives, and so on. Therefore you can always work out how many dominoes of any kind have still to appear. This is very important because it lets you know whether you can block your opponent or he can block you.

Some people do not choose the first player before starting. They take seven dominoes each and the player with the highest double starts. This is done by asking 'Has anyone got the double six?' If everybody says 'No', you ask for the double-five and so on down until you find a double which is in someone's hand. If no one has a double the player with the highest 'six-card' (that is the six-five, six-four and so on down) is the leader. If no one has a double or a 'six' you start on the 'fives', and while it is possible for no one to have the five-four someone must have the five-three. If the answer is still 'No' everyone should show their dominoes and start again.

There are several ways of placing the dominoes and you may find you like one better than the others. In the first the dominoes are placed end to end in one line although you are allowed to turn corners when the line gets near the edges of the table.

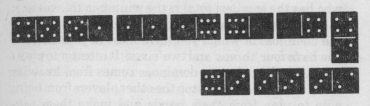

A slight variation on this pattern allows you to place doubles across the line. In most games you only play from the sides of these crosswise doubles but there are a few games (like *Sebastopol* and *Maltese Cross*) where you can play from the ends as well.

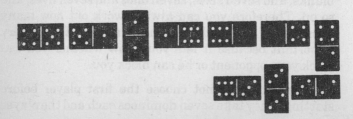

Many people who play the *Block Game* do not let you take dominoes from the boneyard when you cannot go. You just miss your turn and the dominoes in the boneyard are never used. Others say you must take dominoes from the boneyard until you can go or until there are no dominoes left in it.

A very common rule about taking dominoes from the boneyard is that the last two dominoes must be left in it and not taken out. This rule makes it more difficult to work out how to block the game since you do not know the values of the two dominoes in the boneyard.

Another small change that is sometimes made in the rules is that you take only seven dominoes when there are two or three players. In this version, four players take five dominoes each. This is a good idea if more than four players want to join in the game since you can say: five players take four dominoes each, six players take four, and seven or eight players take three each. This does make the game slightly more interesting but if you really want to play with more than four people it is far better to get hold of a double-nine set.

Try all these different ways of playing either separately or together until you find the way of playing that you like best. There is no correct way of playing and the one you enjoy most is obviously the one to play most.

FIVES*   *Two to four players*

This is one of a family of games in which you try to make the ends of the chain of dominoes add up to some number or a multiple of that number. They can be very exciting and make a pleasant change from the normal *Block Game* and its variants.

The first player is chosen as in the *Block Game*, the dominoes are shuffled face down and each player takes seven (if four people are playing they each take six). The remaining dominoes are pushed to one side, still face down, to form the boneyard.

The object of this game is to play dominoes so that the joining ends match and the sum of the pips at the free ends of the chain is five, ten, fifteen, twenty, and so on. That is, so that the sum of the free ends is a multiple of five.

If the ends add up to five, the player of the last domino scores one point; if they add up to ten, he scores two; for fifteen, he scores three and so on.

Doubles go crosswise and both parts of the double are added together to make the score as large as possible.

For example, suppose Francis puts out the six-four as the first domino. The ends of the chain are six and four, which add up to ten. He therefore scores two points.

When Rosemary puts out the six-one, she scores one point because the free ends of the chain (one and four) add up to five.

Margaret, the next player, cannot score but puts out the four-five.

Veronica, in her turn, scores two by playing the one-five.

This leaves the way open for Francis to put out his five-five and score three (the double-five counts as ten and, with the five at the other end, the total is fifteen).

Play goes on like this until one player has no more dominoes left or none of the players can go.

It is usual to play so that if a player cannot go he must take a domino from the boneyard. Of course it is perfectly possible to play the game with any of the rules about the boneyard that are described in the *Block Game*. Try out several different ways of playing before you decide on the way you like best.

You can play each game for itself but it is better to keep the score on a cribbage board or a piece of paper. If you want to do this it is a good idea to have some score for the number of points left in the other players' hands.

One way of doing this is as follows.

If a player has got rid of all his dominoes he gets one point for each five pips in the other players' hands. Any pips that are left over do not count. For example, if Rosemary gets rid of all her dominoes and the pips in the other players' hands add up to eighteen, she will score three points (since eighteen is *three* fives and three over).

The winner is usually the first person to score thirty-one points.

If the game ends because none of the players can go, the winner is the one with the smallest total number of pips in his hand. In this case you add up all the pips on all the dominoes held in the hands, take away the pips held by the winner, and give him one point for each five pips. Any pips that are left over do not count. For example, suppose Margaret has three pips in her hand, Veronica has four, Francis seven and Rosemary eight. Margaret is the winner. The total number of pips is twenty-two. When you take away those held by Margaret you are left with nineteen and she scores three points (nineteen is *three* fives and four over).

All Fives

A variation of *Fives*, which is much more exciting because bigger scores can be made, is called *All Fives* or *Muggins*.

This game is played and scored like *Fives* except that the first player must put out a double. It is usual to start with the highest double in your hand.

After dominoes have been played to each side of the first double (just as in most domino games), players can join dominoes on to the ends of this double if they like. They are not allowed to join on to the ends of any other doubles.

So long as the ends of the first double have not been used the chain has only two ends which are added together to make multiples of five (as in *Fives*). When one end of the first double has been used, there are three free ends to be added together; and when both ends of the first double have been used, there are four ends to be added.

For example, if the dominoes have been put out like this

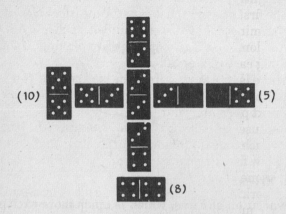

and someone plays the double-six, he will score seven $(12 + 10 + 8 + 5 = 35$, and $35 = 5 \times 7)$.

The origin of the name *Muggins* lies in its only other rule. If a player does not notice that he has made the ends add up to a multiple of five (that is, he does not claim his score) any other player can call 'Muggins' and take the score for himself. If the player calling 'Muggins' has made a mistake, the player he is claiming against scores one point.

All the other rules of the game are the same as those for *Fives*.

The winner is the first player to score sixty-one points (if you are keeping a score). This is once round a cribbage board. If you do not have a cribbage board you can easily keep the score on a piece of paper.

Fives and Threes

This is a development of the game of *Fives* but the rules are slightly different.

The first player is chosen as for the *Block Game*. After the dominoes have been shuffled each player takes seven dominoes if two or three are playing. If four are playing each player takes six.

There is no drawing from the boneyard. If you cannot match one of the free ends of the chain you cannot go and the next player on your left has his turn.

Because you cannot take dominoes from the boneyard it is much more difficult to get rid of all your dominoes. To allow for this anyone who gets rid of all his dominoes scores one point.

In working out the scores during play you have to look out for multiples of both three and five. You get one point if the ends add up to three or five; you get two points if they add up to six or ten; you get three points if they add up to nine. If you can make them add up to fifteen you score eight points – three for the fives and five for the threes.

The winner is the first player to score forty-one points.

Suppose Veronica and Rosemary are going to play. Rosemary has the lead and her seven dominoes are 6-6, 6-3, 5-5, 5-4, 3-3, 3-1, 2-0. She puts out the 6-6. This scores four points because it adds up to twelve (*four* threes).

Veronica has picked up 6-5, 6-2, 6-1, 4-3, 4-0, 2-1, 1-0. She puts out the 6-2. The ends now add up to fourteen, and she does not score.

Rosemary plays the 2-0 and scores four (the ends add up to twelve).

The 6-5 makes the ends add up to five and Veronica scores one.

This lets Rosemary score two points by playing the 5-5 and when Veronica puts out the 0-1 (scoring nothing since the ends add up to eleven), Rosemary scores one by playing the 5-4.

Veronica gets two points by putting out the 1-6 (making the ends add up to ten) and Rosemary replies with the 6-3. This does not score because the ends add up to seven.

By playing the 4-3 so that the ends add up to six Veronica scores two more points. She does not play it so that the ends add up to eight because that would not score.

However, this does let Rosemary score three points by putting out the 3-3 (making the ends add up to nine). Veronica cannot go and so Rosemary can play her last domino. She scores only one point for this since the ends add up to four which is not a multiple of either three or five. If the ends had added up to a scoring total Rosemary would have counted this as well as the one point for last domino.

In all Rosemary has scored fifteen points and Veronica has five.

In the next game Veronica has the lead and they keep on in this way until one of them has scored forty-one points.

You should not lead with either the 6-3 or the 6-6 since this could let your opponent score eight by making the ends add up to fifteen. Much the best domino to start with is the 5-4 since it lets you score three while your opponent can only score two at the most.

As a variation on this game you could try playing *Fives and Threes* as a partnership game for four. In this each player takes five dominoes and must play if they hold a playable domino. The winning pair is the first to reach sixty-one points.

MATADOR *Two to four players*

In this game dominoes are not joined by matching their ends but by making their ends add up to seven. If the six-two is played, any domino with a one on it can be put next to the six, and any domino with a five on it can be put next to the two. For example:

is a possible chain. Doubles are not placed crosswise and are no better than other dominoes.

There are four special dominoes, called *matadors*, which can be played at any time and for them the join does not have to add up to seven. These dominoes are the six-one, the five-two, the four-three and the double-blank. The matadors are the only dominoes that can be played next to a blank.

Matadors are played crossways so that one end blocks the old line of play and the other end is free to start a new line.

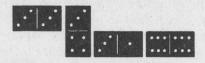

The dominoes are shuffled face down. If two or three people are playing, each one takes six dominoes; if four people are playing, they each take five. The remaining dominoes are pushed to one side, face down, to make the boneyard.

The player with the highest double leads. If no one has a double, the player with the highest domino leads. Each player then takes it in turn, going round to the left from the first player, to place a domino in the chain so that the two joining ends add up to seven.

Once the first domino has been played any player can, when it is his turn, take as many dominoes as he likes from the boneyard, whether he can go or not. But the last two dominoes must always be left asleep in the boneyard.

If a player cannot make the joining ends add up to seven he must play a matador or take dominoes from the boneyard until he can go or until there are only two dominoes left in it. If he has not got a matador and cannot draw from the boneyard he must pass and the player on his left has his turn.

The winner is the first player to get rid of all his dominoes or, if the game is blocked and none of the players can go, the winner is the player who has the smallest total number of pips in his hand. The winner scores the difference between his hand and the total of all the others.

The game is usually played to see who can first score 101.

Matador is a game of skill and the good player watches the dominoes very carefully and counts to see how many of each kind have been played. The dominoes have different values and it is good to play so that your opponent cannot get rid of sixes since these all count in the scoring at the end. For example, if you are playing the six-one matador it is usually best to put it out with the 'six' end free. If you put it with the 'one' end free your opponent can get rid of one of his sixes.

Other valuable dominoes are the blanks since a blank will 'close' one end of the line until a matador is played next to it.

The most valuable of the matadors is the double-blank, which can be played at any time because it is a matador and must be followed by another matador because it leaves a blank free.

Whatever you do, always remember that the last two dominoes in the boneyard are never drawn and you sometimes have to work out, from the way they play, whether your opponents have matadors or not. As in all domino games do not draw too many dominoes from the boneyard. One too many can lose the game.

Matador is much better if played with a double-nine set than with a double-six set. In this case you make the joining ends add up to ten and the matadors are the nine-one, eight-two, seven-three, six-four, double-five and double-blank.

This is an excellent game for four people.

SEBASTOPOL   *Two to seven players*

Sebastopol takes its name from one of the battles of the Crimean War but it is also called *The Star* and *The Fortress* and is probably much older than the name suggests.

The game is usually played by four people but I describe how it can be played by any number up to seven in the variations at the end.

The dominoes are shuffled face down and each player takes seven.

The player who has the double-six puts it face up in the middle of the table. Each player then takes it in turn to join a domino on to this double. This means that at the beginning only sixes can be played either on to the sides or the ends of the double-six and no other dominoes can be played until the 'star' is complete as shown in the diagram.

Once the star has been finished, however, the play is just the same as that for the *Block Game* except that all four ends can be used – so that in our example the next player can put out a one, a two, a three or a four.

The winner is the first player to get rid of all his dominoes.

The game can be played by any number of players from two to seven, as follows.

The dominoes are shuffled face down and a leader is chosen as in the *Block Game*. The dominoes are shuffled again, face down, and each player takes some dominoes. If two or three are playing, they each take seven dominoes; four players take five dominoes each; five take four each; and six or seven take three each.

The player with the highest double puts it out in the middle of the table, face up. If no one has a double the leader takes a domino from the dominoes that have not been taken. If it is a double he plays it; if it is not he keeps it but says 'No'. This tells the next player on his left that he must take a domino from the boneyard. If it is a double he plays it; if it is not he says 'No' and the player on his left has a turn. This goes on until a double is taken from the boneyard, and is played out into the middle of the table.

Once the first double has been played, it has to be turned into a star as was explained above, before the players can match ends.

The first player to get rid of all his dominoes is the winner.

Sebastopol can also be played with the double-nine set and this game is sometimes called *Cyprus*. The star is much more complicated and has eight ends when it is complete.

It is possible to play a game with a double-six set of dominoes in which you have six ends after the star has been made (it should look like the diagram below). Just to make things complicated this game is also called *Cyprus*.

Some people who play *Cyprus* (and even *Sebastopol*) allow dominoes to be played on to the ends before the star is complete. I cannot see why they do this since it ignores the point of making the star in the first place.

MALTESE CROSS*   *Two to four players (best with four)*

The game is usually played by four people but, as with *Sebastopol*, you can change the rules slightly to allow two or three to take part. The game is not very good, however, with more than four players. I will describe the game for four players first.

The dominoes are shuffled face down and each player takes seven. The player who has the double-six puts it face up in the middle of the table. The next player on his left must play a six but can join it on to either side or either end of the double. Suppose he plays the six-two.

The next player, on his left, can either put out a six, which will join on to the double six, or the double-two. Once this double has been played the end is free for other players until a domino is played which ends in a number whose double has not yet been put out. The end is then blocked until the double is played.

Once a double has been played all ends of the same value are open to the players. For example, if you have put out the dominoes to make the pattern

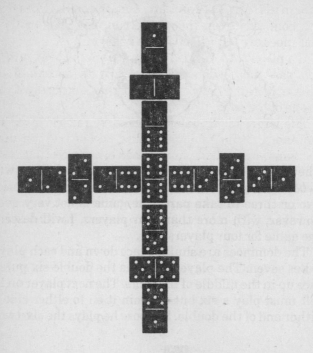

the next player must either put out the double-one or pass. No one can play until the double-one appears. Once it has been put out the players can join on to any end they like, so long as they match ends properly.

If two or three players want to play *Maltese Cross* it is best to choose a leader as in the *Block Game* and then take seven dominoes each. The player with the highest double puts it out in the middle of the table. If there are no doubles the leader chooses a domino from the pile, and if this is a double the game can start. If it is not a double he puts it in his hand and the next player chooses a domino, and so on until a double appears.

After the first domino has been played each player can, in his turn, take as many dominoes as he likes from the boneyard even though he can play. The last two dominoes are left asleep in the boneyard.

If a player has decided to draw from the boneyard he can pass only when there are two dominoes left. Of course, he can, at any time before that, decide to play on to one of the ends.

The winner is the player who first gets rid of all his dominoes. If the game is blocked and no one can play, the winner is the player with the lowest total of pips in his hand.

Maltese Cross can also be played with a double-nine set but it is probably best not to make an eight-pointed star (as for *Cyprus*) but just to use a four-pointed one.

3 BOARD GAMES

There are so many different board games that I can give you details of only a few but I have chosen the ones I feel are most interesting.

You will need to buy or make a board and collect pieces for all these games. If you have a draughts board and draughtsmen, a chess set and a large number of counters (although dried beans are very good) you should be able to play most of the games in this section. There are short descriptions included for each game which tell you how to draw the board, with suggestions for pieces for each game.

The important things to learn about board games are the moves of the pieces and the ways in which to win. You will enjoy the games more if you study these carefully first.

MADELINETTE   *Two players*

This is a very simple board game which is supposed to have been invented in France.

To begin you have to draw the diagram on the left below on a piece of paper or cardboard.

Each player needs three counters – one of them having red ones and the other having white. The counters are placed on the board as in the diagram on the right.

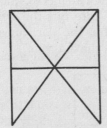
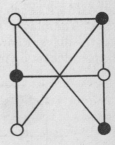

A first player is chosen by tossing a coin and he moves one of his pieces along a line on to the empty central point. The other player then moves one of his pieces on to the new empty point and they go on like this, taking turns to move pieces along lines to empty points, until one player manages to block the other one's move. The player who does this is the winner.

DODGEM *Two players*

This simple-looking little game was invented by Colin Vout. You will find many subtleties when you play it and it is certainly more interesting than noughts and crosses.

The original form of the game is played on a three-by-three board with each player having two pieces, known as 'cars'. The player known as White has the white pieces; the player known as Black has the black ones.

The board is set up initially as in the diagram.

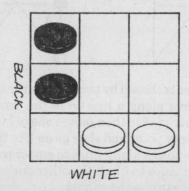

BLACK

WHITE

On his turn a player can move one of his cars either one square to the left, or one to the right, or one square straight forward but only on to an empty square. No more than one car can be on a square at a time.

White makes the first move and then the players take it in turn.

The first player to get both of his cars off the board on the side farthest from him wins the game. In doing this, the player tries to prevent his opponent from getting his cars off the board, but he must always leave him at least one move, since a player who blocks both of his opponent's cars loses.

When you feel you have found out how to play *Dodgem* on the small board, you can make the game more difficult by increasing its size – try playing on a four-by-four board, or a five-by-five and so on. But remember that the bottom left-hand corner must be left empty.

Dodgem is a game full of little traps and you will find that you can be surprised by an expert. It is sometimes better to keep a car on the board rather than push it off as soon as you can. A car on the board blocks your opponent and makes him waste moves by going round it.

NINE MEN'S MORRIS*   *Two players*

This is a very old game that has been played for thousands of years all over the world. It was most popular about five hundred years ago. Monks used to mark out boards for *Nine Men's Morris* in churches and these can still be seen. Very few people play *Nine Men's Morris* today but this is a pity since it is a very good game.

If you are going to play *Nine Men's Morris* you will need to draw a special board. This is quite simple since it is just three squares placed inside one another with the middles of each side joined together by straight lines.

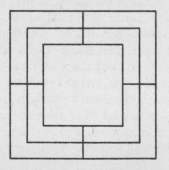

It can easily be drawn on a piece of paper but cardboard is better if you want to keep the board.

You will also need nine pieces for each player. You could use draughts or counters or pebbles, as long as one player has nine pieces of one colour and the other has nine pieces of a different colour. If you are going to use large pieces you will have to draw a big board in order to have enough room to put them on the board.

Playing *Nine Men's Morris* is like playing a mixture of noughts and crosses and *Draughts* If you have played other board games you will know that you usually put your pieces between the lines. *Nine Men's Morris* is different because you have to put your pieces on the places where the lines cross or where they make corners, which I will call points.

In playing the game you take one of the other player's pieces every time you get three of your pieces in a straight line along one of the lines of the board. The other player does the same to you. You each try to leave the other player with only two pieces and the player who first does this is the winner.

You start by taking it in turn to put out your pieces on the points until each player has used up all nine of his men. You can put only one piece on each point.

This is the first part of the game. During this part each player tries to put out his pieces so that he has three in a straight line along one of the lines of the board. If a player can put three of his men so that they make a line he can take one of the other player's pieces from the board. *But* he must not take a piece that is in a line, unless there are no other pieces to take.

Either player can, when it is his turn, put a piece on the board which will stop the other player getting three in a line.

The first part of the game ends when the players have

put out all nine of their men on the board. In the second part of the game each player tries to win pieces from the other by moving his men so that he gets three in a line. You can move only one piece at a time from one point to the next along a line. Black could move from the corner either to the right or down. White could move in any one of the four ways marked.

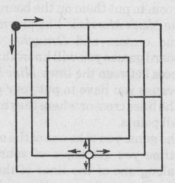

When a player moves his pieces so that three of them make a line along one of the lines of the board, he can take one of the pieces belonging to the other player. As before, he cannot take a piece that is in a line of three unless there are no other pieces to take.

The second part of the game ends when one of the players has only three pieces left. This player is then allowed to move a piece from one point to any other point on the board. He does not have to move along the lines. (But he cannot, of course, move to a point with a piece on it already.) The other player still has to move along the lines.

Each player still tries to get his pieces to lie three in a line.

If both players have only three pieces they are each allowed to move by jumping from one point to another and they do not have to move along the lines.

As soon as one player is left with only two pieces, he has lost.

MU-TORERE *Two players*

This game comes from New Zealand where it is played by the Maoris, but nobody knows whether it is a very old game or not – it was not written about before 1917.

The board used for the game is an eight-pointed star with each point joined on to a circle in the centre. The circle in the middle is called the 'putahi' and the circles on the ends of the arms, where the men are placed to start, are called 'kewai'.

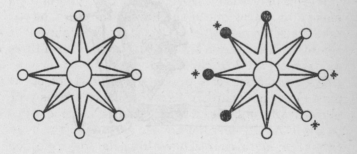

Each player has four men and they are placed on four kewai which are next to each other, as in the second diagram.

The object of the game is to make it impossible for the other player to move.

A man can be moved from one of the kewai to the next, if it is empty. A man can also be moved from the putahi to one of the kewai. Lastly, a man can be moved from one of the kewai to the putahi but this can only be done if one of the kewai next to it (or both of them) has an enemy piece on it.

This last rule means that you cannot start the game by moving one of the pieces marked with a star in the second diagram.

The game can go on for a long time between two good players but it is simple enough for young people to play with enjoyment.

GOBANG* *Two players*

The national game of Japan is I-go which is just as difficult as chess, although this makes it very interesting to learn and play. The game of *Gobang* is played by children in Japan on the I-go board and is quite difficult enough to make a good game.

You can buy I-go boards and pieces but it is probably better to make one yourself first to see how you like the game before doing so. An I-go board is a large square with eighteen small squares on each side. Drawing it can be difficult because of the large number of squares but care and a long rule should solve that problem.

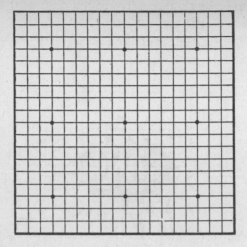

Pieces are another difficulty – you will need a hundred for each player – but small buttons or pebbles of different colours can be used. It does not matter if they are not all of the same shape so long as the colours are distinct – you must know which are your pieces and which are your opponent's.

The object of the game is to get five of your men in a line, either going from side to side, or up and down, or diagonally.

The players take turns to put out one of their pieces on to any of the small squares of the board. The pieces cannot be moved once they have been put down until each player has used up all of his pieces.

When both players have used up all their pieces (you can only get to this stage when you are quite skilled at the game – you will usually find that one player gets five men in a line quite quickly) they are allowed to move one man at a time, on their turn, one square either up and down or from side to side. Men cannot be moved diagonally.

The first player to get five of his men next to each other and in a straight line is the winner.

The diagram below shows a game which has been won by White.

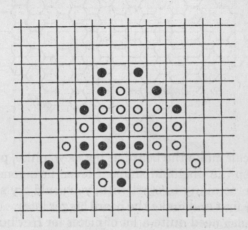

HEX*   *Two players*

This intriguing game was invented by the Dane, Piet Hein, just over thirty years ago and quickly became very popular in Denmark. It has now been introduced to all the other parts of the world but you may have some difficulty in finding a shop that sells the boards and pieces.

Drawing the board is also quite difficult, but you do not need to have all the hexagons of the same size, nor all the lines straight. I once found some cloth which had been printed with hexagons as a pattern and this, when cut up and stuck on to some cardboard, made a very good hex board.

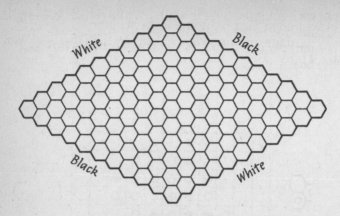

You can make the board as big as you like, provided you keep the diagonal shape. Eleven hexagons across may be too many to start with; you could try seven or eight at first and make the board bigger later.

You also need quite a lot of pieces for *Hex* but if you have tried to play *Gobang* you will have more than enough. Remember you need pieces of two different colours – and make sure they will fit inside the hexagons you have drawn.

One player uses the white pieces (and is called White) while the other uses the black pieces (and is called Black).

Two of the opposite sides of the board are labelled 'Black' and the other two are labelled 'White'. These sides belong to the player whose name they bear. The hexagons at the corners of the diamond belong to both players.

The object of the game is to put out a line of stepping stones from one of your sides to the other. It does not have to be a straight line but can curl and twist about as much as you like – the only thing to watch out for is that it must not have any gaps in it. The diagram below shows a complete line made by White which goes right across the board. Because he has put a piece in the corner hexagon it counts as being on the White side of the board.

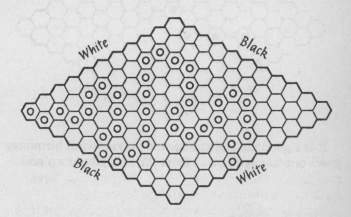

One player is chosen to start and puts one of his pieces on to any hexagon he chooses. The other player then puts out one of his pieces as he likes, and they go on like this, in turn, until one of them manages to make a complete line. The first player to do this wins.

The best first move is to put a piece on the central hexagon, if there is one, or as close to the centre as possible.

In trying to make a line do not just play on the hexagon next to the last man you put down. If your opponent sees that you are doing this he will easily block you – and win. It is far better to put your pieces on the hexagon one away from the last one you played in. If you can get a broken line like this from one side of the board to the other (as in the next diagram) then your opponent cannot stop you filling it in.

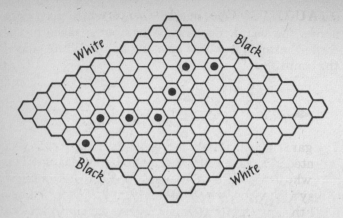

It is a good idea for the second player to put his pieces down one hexagon away from the first player's pieces.

DRAUGHTS* (Checkers)   *Two players*

The game which was to be turned into *Draughts* was invented in France about seven hundred years ago. The man who invented it was probably trying to find out how to play alquerque on a chess board but his invention has lived through many changes to become the game we know today.

Draughts is played on a square board of sixty-four squares (eight to a side) which are usually coloured black and white alternately. The same board is used for playing chess.

Each player has twelve pieces, or men, which are usually flat round bits of wood. Twelve of the men are of one colour (normally black) and the other twelve are of a different colour (normally white).

The player who has the twelve black pieces is called Black and the other player is called White.

If you do not have a board you can easily draw one on a piece of paper or cardboard. The lines do not have to be completely straight, and the squares do not all have to be of the same size. Just make sure there is enough room on each little square for the pieces you are going to use and that there are eight little squares in each of the lines. Paint the squares in any two colours you like.

Pieces can be more difficult but quite good ones can be made by sawing an old broom handle into twenty-four flat pieces and colouring twelve of them. Counters, buttons or bottle tops could also be used – I once played

Draughts on a checked towel with slices of carrot and sugar cubes for the pieces.

Black

White

To play a game of *Draughts* you place the board so that the double black corner is on your right.

One of the players picks up a black piece and a white one and, behind his back, hides one in his right hand and the other in his left. He then stretches out his two fists to the other player, taking care that he cannot see the colours of the draughtsmen. The other player chooses a fist and will play with the pieces of the same colour as the piece that was in it.

Black always moves first.

If you are going to play more than one game, choose the colours for the first game as just described and then take it in turns to be Black.

When you have worked out who is going to start, you put out the men on the board. The twelve black men go on the twelve black squares nearest to the player who is Black and the twelve white men go on the twelve black squares nearest to White.

The game is played on the black squares only. This means that the pieces move diagonally to the right or the left. Men can only move one square at a time and can only move forwards, that is away from the player who is moving them.

If a man reaches one of the four squares on the far side of the board, it becomes a 'king' and can move forwards and backwards (but still only on the black squares and only one square at a time). Pieces are taken off the board during the game and it is usual to place one of these on top of a piece that has become a king, making a pile of two draughtsmen. Putting this second piece on top of the first is called 'crowning'.

The object of the game is to take all the other player's pieces or to trap him so that he cannot move.

Men can only move on to squares that are empty. If

the piece that is in the way of a move belongs to the other player, and the black square beyond it is empty, then you *must* jump over the enemy piece into the empty square. The enemy man is then taken off the board.

If a man can make more than one jump, one after the other, either in a straight line or in a zig-zag, it must make all of them and take all the pieces it jumps over. Of course, a man can only jump forwards. A king can jump backwards and forwards.

If a man jumps into one of the last four squares, where it is crowned, its move must end there. It cannot jump over any of the other player's pieces until it is its turn again.

Before you make any move look carefully at the board to see if you can take any of the other player's men. And when you have finished your move, look carefully to see whether he can take any of your men. You must do this because, if you have not seen that you could take a man on your turn, the other player can 'huff' you before making his move.

Let us pretend that you have finished your move and did not see that you could take one of his men. He can make you take back your last move and jump over the pieces you did not see. Or he can 'huff' you by removing from the board the man (or king) that should have jumped. Or he can do nothing at all. Of course, if the other player does not take some of your pieces you have the same choice.

A player who does not take as many pieces on his turn as he could (for example, making only two jumps when he could have made three) can be huffed. But if a player has to choose between several different jumps which would take different numbers of pieces it does not matter which move he chooses.

Huffing does not count as a move. 'A huff and a move' go together.

Draughts is quite a simple game since it has very few rules and all the pieces move in the same way. Despite its simplicity it is possible to plan your moves in *Draughts* in much the same way as you do in chess but there is no real need to show you all the different positions that can arise. However, I can give you some general advice.

It is usually better to move your men to the centre of the board. If you move them to the edges they lose half their power to attack, while in the middle they can attack in all directions. And when you are moving your men be careful not to allow the other player to take two of your men for one of his. To stop this you must move up your other pieces.

Always look over the board carefully before making your move and try to work out what will happen because of each move before you make it.

When you have won more of the other player's pieces than you have lost of your own, you should try to increase your advantage by exchanging pieces, that is making him take one of yours in such a way that you take one of his on the next move. You must be careful when doing this, however, because you can weaken your position.

Play slowly at first and always try to work out what plan your opponent is trying to follow. Remember that he is trying to trap you, just as you are trying to trap him.

Try to keep your men as close together as possible, especially at the end of the game. The fewer men you have, the closer together you should keep them.

Draughts has several rules which I have not mentioned because very young children cannot be expected to obey them all the time. But they should be obeyed by older players, for the sake of politeness and good manners as much as anything else. They include such obvious things as not pointing over the board, nor trying to stop the other player seeing it properly. You should not shout or sing so that he cannot think properly, either. If you want to go out of the room while the game is still going on, you should ask his permission first.

You must not finger the pieces. If you touch a piece, you must move it unless you have said 'I am just adjusting' *before* you touch the piece – and it is better to say it before your hand is above the board. The first time a piece is touched without anything being said, the player should be warned; and the second time he should lose the game.

A man which is moved so that any part of it is over the corner of the square on which it is standing, must continue moving in the same direction if this is possible. Very young players can, of course, be allowed to 'see what will happen' by actually moving pieces about on the board. Older players must learn how to imagine the results of their actions.

Any move is over as soon as the player's hand is taken off the man. If he then realizes, for example, that he could have taken more pieces in the same move, it is too late and the other player can huff him, if he wants to.

A player could, if he felt nasty, hold up the game by waiting for a long time before making his move. The rules say that if one player has waited without making a move for five minutes, the other player can call 'Time'. The first player must then move one of his pieces before another minute has passed. If he does not do so then he has lost the game.

If a player must take one or more of the other player's pieces and there is only one way to do so, he must not delay for more than a minute. If he does, the other player can call 'Time' and, if the move is not made before another minute has passed, the first player has lost.

Of course these rules about the time which can be taken over a move, and the penalties if they are not obeyed, are for expert players and should be ignored with the young. However, it is a good idea to play the game as nearly as possible according to the strict rules.

Remember that the player who does not obey the rules loses the game.

POLISH DRAUGHTS** *Two players*

Polish Draughts is one of the world's greatest games. It is well worth while taking the trouble of making a board and pieces to play it. Until you have done so, you cannot understand how different it is from the games played on the usual chessboard.

Polish Draughts is supposed to have been invented by a Pole in Paris in the early eighteenth century. It is played on a square board of a hundred squares with twenty pieces on each side. At the beginning of the game they are arranged as in the diagram.

The men move diagonally forward, one square at a time, as in ordinary *Draughts*.

The men take forwards and backwards by jumping over a man of the other colour and landing on the empty square beyond.

When a man's move stops on the last row it is crowned and becomes a king (or a queen, if you prefer it). If a man lands on the last row and can still take more of the other player's pieces, it must do so and is not crowned until its move ends on the last row.

The kings move diagonally any number of empty squares, just like the bishop in chess. The king takes by jumping over an enemy piece and can land any number of squares beyond it.

When you have a choice between taking different numbers of men, you must take the larger number or the larger pieces. If you can take a man or a king, you must take the king.

When a king is taking several pieces one after the other all the pieces it has jumped over are left on the board until the end of the move. They are then taken off. A piece that has been jumped once cannot be jumped over again. If you find it difficult to remember which pieces have been jumped and which have not, put a marker on the ones which have been jumped – you could use little counters or dead matches, anything that is small and will not leave a mark on the draughtsmen.

This ban on jumping twice is only true of squares which have the other player's pieces on them. Empty squares can be jumped over as often as you like in the same move.

The king in *Polish Draughts* is much stronger than the king in ordinary *Draughts*. This means that getting a king quickly is very important, and, once you have got it, you must try not to lose it.

Giving the exchange – giving one of your men and taking off one of the other player's – is far more important also. The other player may be trying to arrange for a long string of jumps. To stop him you must push up one of your men so that he has to take it, ruining his plan.

Or you may want to trap the other player, by making him take one of your men so that you can take several of his.

The position with two men of the same colour separated by an empty square happens more often in *Polish Draughts* than in ordinary *Draughts*. Of course, if you put one of your men between them, one of the men must be taken because they cannot both escape at the same time. Very often this position offers several jumps on each side.

But do not push your piece into the gap and think the other player has made a mistake. It is probably a trap and you should try to work out what he is planning to do.

At the end of the game, when there are only a few men left on the board, try to get them as close together as possible. They can then lend each other some strength.

Any mistake, even the smallest, at the end of the game is usually fatal. The kings are so strong that it is worth giving up two or three men if you can get a king. But you must always watch and see that the king will be safe and will be able to take as many men as you have given up. A skilful player will try to trap a king as soon as he has been crowned.

Polish Draughts can also be played as a 'losing' game and you will find that this form is much better than the 'losing' form of ordinary *Draughts*.

If you want to try an interesting variation you could let the kings move like the queen in chess, instead of just like the bishop. Of course, the king can land only on black squares, as in the diagram above, but you should let it have the 'long move' in all directions so that it can jump on to any empty square beyond one of the other player's pieces. This game (called *Babylonian*) was also invented in France in the early eighteenth century but has since died out.

You could also make the board still bigger and play on a twelve by twelve board of 144 squares. You will need thirty men for each side in this game but the rules should be exactly like those of *Polish Draughts*. This game is played in Canada as *le jeu de dames canadien*, *Canadian Draughts*, but it has been played in other parts of the world.

FOX AND GEESE* *Two players*

This game is only one of a whole family of games played all over the world, and called many different names. In all of them one player has more pieces than the other, and each player moves his pieces in different ways.

You can play a simple form of the game on an ordinary chess board, using draughtsmen as the pieces.

One player has four white pieces – which are called 'geese' – while the other player has one black piece – the 'fox'.

The geese all start the game on the four black squares nearest to White. The fox can be put anywhere on the board that Black pleases.

The geese move like the men in ordinary *Draughts* – one square forward diagonally, always keeping on the black squares. The fox can move diagonally backwards or forwards, one square, like the king in *Draughts* (of course, it also stays on the black squares). It cannot, however, jump over the geese – there is no taking in this game.

When Black has put the fox on the board, White moves one of the geese. The fox then moves and they go on like this, in turn, until either the fox gets through the line of geese, or the geese trap the fox so that it cannot move.

As you will quickly learn, the geese can always win if they keep together and in as straight a line across the board as possible. If they leave a hole in their line it is very easy for the fox to slip through.

Sometimes the game is played with White having twelve men and Black only one. In this game the white pieces start on the first three rows of black squares nearest to White (just as in *Draughts*) while the Black piece starts in one of the black corner squares on the other side of the board. The white pieces are sometimes called 'goats' and the black piece is called the 'wolf' – so that the game is *Wolf and Goats*.

The goats move like ordinary draughtsmen and the wolf moves like a king. But, unlike *Fox and Geese* described above, the wolf is able to jump over the goats and take them off the board – the goats cannot jump over the wolf.

The wolf tries to break through the goats, and the goats try to trap the wolf so that it cannot move. As in *Fox and Geese* the white pieces should win.

Fox and Geese is also played on special boards and the best of these is probably that shown on the left below. In this game you play on the points where lines meet, not in the spaces between the lines.

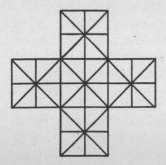
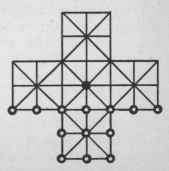

You can play this form of *Fox and Geese* on a solitaire board, if you draw in the lines joining the holes.

White, who has the geese, puts out his thirteen men as shown in the right-hand diagram on p. 145 while Black, the fox, usually puts his man on the centre spot.

Both the fox and the geese move in the same way – one step along any line on to the next point, if it is empty. Two men cannot stand on the same point. The move can be forwards or backwards.

The geese cannot take the fox but the fox can jump over a goose which is next to it, if the square immediately beyond the goose is empty. The fox can make more than one jump on one turn, so long as it lands on an empty point and is next to an enemy piece.

The fox wins if it takes so many geese that they cannot trap it; the geese win if they can trap the fox so that it cannot move.

LASCA* *Two players*

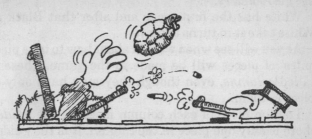

This exciting game was invented by Edward Lasker, a very famous chess player. One of the best things about the game comes from the sudden changes in the number of pieces that each player has.

It is played on a square board of forty-nine squares (that is, seven squares by seven squares) which are coloured black and white like a chess board, with a white square at each corner. You play on the white squares only.

You do not have to make a special board since you can use an ordinary chess board and cover the squares along two of the edges.

Each player has eleven pieces – the one who has the white pieces will be called White, the one with the black pieces will be called Black. The pieces must be flat so that they can be piled on top of each other. I use wooden draughtsmen but any flat counters would do. One side of each piece is marked – with a spot of paint or a small hole. When the unmarked side is on top, the piece is called a *soldier*. When the marked side is on top, the piece is called an *officer*.

At the beginning of the game all of White's eleven pieces are put on the eleven white squares nearest to him. They all start as *soldiers*. Black's eleven pieces are placed on the eleven white squares nearest to him and are also *soldiers*.

White has the first move and after that Black and White take it in turns to move.

As you will see when we talk about how to take pieces, 'piles' of pieces will be made in the game. These are called *columns*, even though they may have only one piece in them.

The top piece of each column is called the *guide*. If there is only one piece in the column, it is the guide. If the top piece is white, it is a white column and is moved by White. If the top piece is black, it is a black column and is moved by Black.

A column guided by a soldier moves diagonally forward, that is away from the player moving it, from one white square to the next, just as the men move in ordinary *Draughts*.

When a column guided by a soldier reaches the row farthest away from the player moving it, the guide (the top piece of the pile) is turned over so that it becomes an *officer*. Columns guided by officers can be moved backwards or forwards one square, like the king in ordinary *Draughts*, on to an empty square.

The interest of the game is caused by the way in which you take the other player's pieces. *In taking you only take the guide*. If a column guided by a piece of the other colour is on a square next to one of your columns, and the square beyond it is empty, you can take it (just as you could take it in ordinary *Draughts*). You take men in *Lasca* by putting your column on top of the other column, picking up your column together with the other column's guide, and moving this (larger) column on to the empty square.

For example, suppose you have a column of three white pieces next to a column of two black pieces, as in the diagram. You take the guide of the black column with you when you jump and you end up with a column of four pieces – three white pieces on top of a black piece. The other black piece, the one that was on the bottom of the old black column, stays on its square.

If your column was guided by an officer it could then jump back over this piece, picking it up, and land on the square it started from. It would then be a column of five pieces – three white ones on top of two black ones.

An officer is not turned over when it is taken. It goes into the pile capturing it, as an officer, but does not have any power to move until all the pieces on top of it have been taken and it becomes a guide.

You will see that a column is made up of a set of pieces of one colour on top of a set of pieces of the other colour. You cannot have the pieces arranged black-white-black-white in a single column.

If you can take one of the other player's pieces you must take it. If you can jump over several pieces, one after the other, you must do so. A move stops only when there are no more pieces to jump over or a soldier reaches the farthest row and becomes an officer. Even if the new officer could jump over some of the other player's pieces it must wait until the other player has made a move.

If you have to choose between different jumps you can make any one you like but you *must* choose one of them.

You win the game by making it impossible for the other player to move. You can do this by taking all his pieces. This means that all the columns on the board will have your pieces on top. You can also do it by blocking all his moves.

In playing *Lasca* you must realize that the best way to take the other player's pieces is to let him jump over one of your pieces and then to jump over the new column yourself. In this way he loses a piece and you do not lose any. You can work out how you are getting on in the game by seeing how many columns the other player has and how many you have. You can then work out how these numbers will change after a particular set of moves. The player with the greater number of pieces is usually winning.

Remember that it is only the top piece of the column that is taken by a soldier and this means that the next piece becomes the guide of the column that is left behind. Also try to remember which of your columns have got your enemy's officers in them, and which of his columns have your officers in them. It is possible for you to capture one of his 'soldier columns' and leave behind one of his officers, which could win the game for him. Of course, you might capture one of his columns and leave behind one of your own officers.

This constant change in the number of pieces on each side is one of the most exciting parts of the game. At one moment you are losing – you only have five columns and he has eight. One move from you and, suddenly, you have six columns and he has five.

PASTA*   *Two players*

I first came across the game of *Pasta* in a computer magazine in 1974 where it was stated that the inventor was an American called Pastor. It is a very simple game to play but allows for the use of a great deal of cunning.

Pasta is played on a square board of sixty-four squares (eight on a side) which is usually coloured black and white alternately – the board used for playing chess.

Each player has twelve pieces, or men, which must be flat since the pieces are piled on top of each other during the game. Twelve of the men are of one colour (normally white) and the other twelve are of a different colour (normally black).

The player with the white pieces will be called White, the one with the black pieces will be called Black.

At the beginning of the game the board is placed with the double black corner on your right. White's twelve pieces are placed on the twelve black squares nearest to him and the twelve black ones are placed on the black squares nearest to Black.

White always has the first move, and after that Black and White take it in turn to move.

As happens in the game of *Lasca*, 'piles' of pieces are made during the game. These are usually called columns even though they may have only one piece in them. The columns will be made up of a number of pieces of one colour either by themselves or on top of a number of pieces of the other colour. Colours will not alternate in a column.

A column consisting of a man by himself or one man on top of a number of pieces of the other colour is a *soldier* column.

A column consisting of two or more men of one colour either by themselves or on top of a number of pieces of the other colour is an *officer* column.

If the top piece or pieces are white, the column belongs to White and is moved by him. If the top piece or pieces are black, it is a black column and is moved by Black.

A soldier column moves diagonally forward on to an empty square, that is away from the player moving it, from one black square to the next, just as the men move in ordinary *Draughts*.

An officer column can move diagonally backward or forward on to an empty square, from one black square to the next, just as the kings move in *Draughts*.

The main difference in the game of *Pasta* comes from the way you take the other player's pieces. *In taking you only take the top piece*. If a column guided by a piece of the other colour is on a square next to one of your columns, and the square beyond it is empty, you can take it (just as in ordinary *Draughts*). You take men in *Pasta*, just as in *Lasca*, by putting your column on top of the other column, picking up your column together with the top piece of the other column, and moving the (larger) column on to the empty square. Of course, if the column you are capturing only contains one piece, it counts as the top piece of the column.

For example, suppose you have a column of one white piece on top of a black piece next to a column of two black pieces, as in the diagram. You take the top piece of the black column with you when you jump and end up with a column of three pieces – a white piece on top of two black

ones. The other black piece, the one that was on the bottom of the old black column, stays on its square.

If your column had two white pieces on top of a black piece – the officer column – it would still be an officer after it had made the jump and could jump back again to its original square, taking the remaining black piece. It would end up as two white pieces on top of three black ones.

As you can see from these examples, officers can come and go during the course of the game.

If you can take one of the other player's pieces, you must take it. If you can jump over several pieces, one after the other, you must do so. A move only stops when there are no more pieces to jump over.

If you have to choose between different jumps, you can make any one you like, but you must make one of them.

You win the game by ending a move with one of your pieces on the row furthest away from you. In the next diagram White wins by jumping as shown – because his piece is a soldier column it cannot jump out again.

154

BLACK

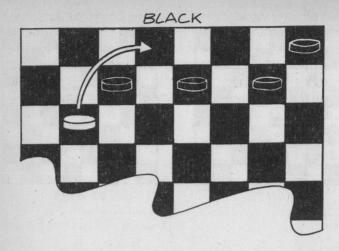

In the next diagram, Black cannot win on his move, because the officer column has to jump out again and does not end its move on the farthest row.

WHITE

In playing *Pasta*, just as in playing *Lasca*, you capture
your opponent's pieces by letting him jump over one of
yours and then jumping over the new column yourself.
This means that he loses a piece and you do not lose any.

In *Pasta* the player with the greater number of pieces
is usually winning but the numbers keep changing and
a few clever moves can often turn the game round
completely.

REVERSI* *Two players*

Reversi was invented about a hundred years ago and two men claimed the honour (and the royalties). Their battles make a very interesting story but the game is even better. It is one of the best games that can be played on a chess board.

To play *Reversi* you need sixty-four pieces which have different colours on opposite sides – black and white, or black and red. If you cannot buy these pieces you can make some for yourself by colouring one side of a piece of cardboard and then cutting out sixty-four small pieces. The pieces do not have to be round, or all the same size or shape. They just need to have different colours on each side.

You can make better pieces by cutting an old broom handle into sixty-four pieces and painting one side black and the other white. Another way of making pieces for *Reversi* is to buy a lot of counters of two different colours and then glue them together in pairs.

If you try the game with cardboard pieces first you can decide whether you think it interesting enough to make better pieces.

One player takes thirty-two pieces and turns them

white side up. We shall call him White. The other player, Black, turns his pieces black side up.

You choose which player will be Black for the first game by tossing a coin or in any other way. After the first game you take it in turns to be Black.

The object of the game is to have as many as possible of your pieces on the board when the game ends.

Black begins by putting one of his pieces on one of the four middle squares. White puts one of his pieces on another middle square. Black then puts his second piece on a third middle square and White puts his second piece on the last middle square. These four squares must be filled first. Experts always start by filling them in as in the diagram below but you do not have to follow them.

After the four middle squares have been filled the players take it in turn to put out pieces one at a time. Each piece must be placed on a square next to one that has an enemy piece on it, either straight up and down, or straight across, or diagonally. It must also trap some of the enemy's pieces between itself and another piece of the same colour with no spaces at any point. On the diagram at the top of the next page Black could play on any of the squares marked *B* and White could play on any of the squares marked *W*.

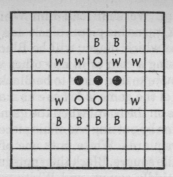

The enemy piece, or pieces, between the two pieces at each end are 'captured' by turning them over so that the whole line shows the same colour. The pieces do not move from one square to another but they can be turned over many times during a game.

If you capture more than one line of pieces by putting out your piece they are all turned over. For example, if Black plays on the shaded square he will capture six pieces – a line of one, a line of two and a line of three pieces.

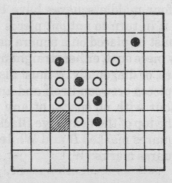

When pieces are turned over they sometimes complete a line. No pieces are captured by this. You can only capture pieces by putting out a man on your turn.

You may find that you cannot make any legal move. If this happens you miss a turn and you keep on missing your turn until you can make a legal move.

The game ends when all sixty-four pieces have been placed on the board, or when both players cannot move. The winner is the player who has most pieces showing his colour on the board at the end of the game.

In playing *Reversi* it is best to stay inside the central sixteen squares for as long as possible and the best squares to put pieces on are those on the long diagonals (shaded in the diagram below). The first player to have to go outside these sixteen central squares often loses.

Outside this central block of squares the most valuable squares are the corners and the squares next but one to them along the edge of the board (shaded in the diagram).

While you should try to capture these squares for yourself you must try to stop your opponent getting them and in particular you should not play on the squares marked *A* in the diagram.

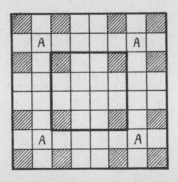

Reversi is a fascinating game but you may find it is too difficult because of the size of the board. If this is so, you should try to play the game on a four-by-four or six-by-six board. In both these forms of the game you must put the first four pieces on the middle four squares just as in the full-sized game.

4 DICE GAMES

Dice are little cubes of bone, plastic or wood. Each face is given a different number and the numbers are usually 1, 2, 3, 4, 5 and 6. These numbers are marked with dots using the same patterns as are on dominoes. The numbers are arranged on dice so that 1 and 6, 2 and 5, and 3 and 4 are opposite each other.

Dice is the plural and means two or more; if you have only one it is called a die, though most people incorrectly use 'dice' for one.

In playing with dice people often use a dice cup but this is not necessary. You must, however, have a level place on to which the dice can be thrown. It should be as clear as possible of all obstacles so that the dice cannot be caught and allowed to balance on edge. The dice must be able to land flat on one side so that it is obvious which side is the top. The score on the top face of each die is the one that is taken for all dice games.

If the dice do not all land with one face of each flat on the playing area, all dice must be thrown again and not just those that were balanced on their edges.

BEETLE *Two or more players (the game gets slow with more than six)*

This is one of the best family games and it is the source of much riotous laughter, especially from the younger players.

The game only needs one die but each player must be given a piece of paper and a pencil so that he can draw his 'beetle'. The die can be an ordinary one but it is possible to buy a special die for this game. You could make one easily from a piece of wood or a lump of sugar (but make sure that it is a cube before you begin).

If you are going to use an ordinary die you must make out a table which shows which part of the beetle each number stands for. For example,

1 Body
2 Head
3 Legs
4 Eyes
5 Feelers
6 Tail

Of course, if you are using a special die it will be marked B (for body), H (for head), L (for legs), E (for eyes), F (for feelers) and T (for tail).

It is best to let the youngest player have first turn.

The players then take it in turn to throw the die, having one throw at each turn. No one can start to draw his beetle until he has thrown a body (or the number that stands for body). If the first player does not get a body he must pass the die to the player on his left who will try to get one on his turn.

Once a player has thrown a body he draws an oval on his piece of paper and on his next turn tries to throw for a head, or a tail which he can join on to the body he has drawn. If he throws legs he can only draw the three legs on one side of the beetle's body and must wait until he throws legs again before he can draw those on the other side.

Feelers and eyes cannot be put in until the head has been joined on to the body and only one feeler and one eye can be drawn at a time.

Each player takes his turn and each time he throws a part of the beetle that he can use he draws it on the paper in front of him. In some games you are allowed to have an extra turn each time you can add to your drawing but you may find that you do not like this variation.

The first person to draw a complete beetle is the winner and he scores thirteen points – one for each part (a body, a head, a tail, two eyes, two feelers and six legs). Each other player scores one point for each part he has been able to draw.

You can play so that the scores from each game are added together and say that the first person to reach fifty-one is the winner.

PIG *Two or more players*

Although this is one of the simplest dice games it is also one of the most exciting. It has the advantage that it can be played with only one die.

Each player throws the die in turn. The player who throws the lowest number begins the game – if several people get the same low number they throw the die amongst themselves to see who gets the lowest number on the second throw. If this again is a draw, they throw again until one of them is chosen.

The starter then throws the die and remembers his score. He throws the die again and adds this new score to his first score. He keeps on doing this as long as he likes, but if he throws a 1 he loses all his score for that turn and must pass the die to the player on his left. Of course, he can stop whenever he likes and keep the points that he has scored. When he stops he gives the die to the player on his left.

The next player throws in his turn until he decides to stop or until he has thrown a 1, whichever comes first. And so on round the table.

The scores for each turn are added up and the winner is the first player to reach 101.

CENTENNIAL *Two or more players (becomes very slow with more than eight)*

This is an exciting race game which is enjoyed by people of every age.

Before you can begin you must draw, on a piece of paper or wood, a long oblong cut up into twelve sections. You then number each of the sections with the numbers from 1 to 12.

1	2	3	4	5	6	7	8	9	10	11	12

Each player is given a counter which everybody knows belongs to him.

Each player throws three dice (if you do not have three dice you can throw one die three times remembering the scores you get). The player throwing the largest total sum is the one who starts the game.

The first player throws the three dice again. He cannot put his counter on the board until he has thrown a 1. If none of the three dice shows a 1 on their top faces, he loses his turn and must give the dice to the player on his left. This second player then tries to throw a 1, and if he fails he passes the dice to the player on his left and so on round the table.

As soon as a player has thrown a 1, he puts his counter on the section marked 1. He cannot move it on to the section marked 2 until he throws a 2 or two 1s (1 + 1 = 2).

Of course, on each throw you might find that you can use more than one die at a time. Suppose you are starting and throw a 1, a 2 and a 4. You can put your counter on the first space because of the 1. You can move it to the second space because of the 2; then on the third space because 1 + 2 = 3; on to the fourth space because of the 4; on to the fifth space because 1 + 4 = 5; on to the sixth space because 2 + 4 = 6; and finally on to the seventh space because 1 + 2 + 4 = 7. You must always look out for the chance to use each die more than once to move as far along the track as possible.

Each player takes his turn to throw until one of them has managed to make his counter travel from 1 to 12 and back again to 1.

Watch the other players carefully when they are throwing because if one of them throws a number that he needs, and does not use it, you can claim it for yourself. Of course, you can only claim numbers that you can use straightaway.

FIFTY   *Two or more players*

A very simple game which only needs two dice.

The players take it in turn to throw the two dice on to the table. You can only score when the pip values on the two dice are the same – two 1s, two 2s and so on.

Two 6s count for 25 points.

All other doubles except two 3s count for 5 points.

If you are unfortunate enough to throw two 3s you lose all the score you have made.

The first player to reach a total of 50 is the winner.

CRICKET*   *One or two players*

This dice game imitates the outdoor game. You need only one die and a lot of patience since it can go on for a long time.

Before you begin, each player decides on a team of eleven men and writes their names down the left-hand side of a lined piece of paper.

The players throw the die to see who gets the higher score and bats first.

The player whose team is batting throws the die and scores runs opposite the name of the first batsman on his list for each throw of 1, 2, 3, 4, or 6. It is assumed that two men are batting at any one time and, since they run between the wickets to score, when an odd number is run the player at the batting end changes. For even scores the batting player remains the same.

Every six throws (just as at the end of an over) the batting man stops scoring and the other batsman who is batting with him begins to score. The only time this does not happen is when an odd score is made on the last throw before the change – in that case the batting man stays the same.

Whenever a 5 is thrown, this counts as an appeal and the die is thrown again by the other player. The result of the appeal depends on his throw.

1 – No ball. The 'batsman' throws the die again and scores as many runs as it shows. If it shows 1, 2, 4 or 6 the batsmen do not change over. If it shows 3 they do. A 5 scores 1 but the batsmen do not cross.

A no ball does not count as one of the six throws of the over.

2 – Not out. The scoring batsman does not change but no score is made. The throw counts as one of the six balls of the over.

3 – Scoring batsman is out: 'Bowled'.

4 – Scoring batsman is out: 'Caught'.

5 – Scoring batsman is out: 'LBW'.

6 – Scoring batsman is out: 'Stumped'.

When a batsman is out, his score is added up and written down on the right of the paper.

The next throw is scored to the next batsman to come in, unless the last batsman was out to the last throw of an over. If this happens, the batsman who was already in scores to the first throw of the next over.

When ten of his batsmen are out the first player's side is out and his total score (including that of the not-out man and any 'extras' from no balls) is added up.

The other player then tries to get a bigger score on his turn, before ten of his men are out. The game ends as soon as the first score is passed or all ten of his men are out.

You can play that each side is allowed two innings, taking turns, and that it is the total over the two innings which counts. In this case it is usual to say that if the first side scores 150 more runs than the second side in the first innings, then the second side must bat before the first when batting for the second time.

In the example below I have shown the ends of overs by the small triangle above the dots (you do not show these when you are playing).

Grace :	1·3·4·6·3·4·3·3·6	L.B.W	3 3
Hutton :	6	Bowled	6
Bradman:	6·4·4·6·1·1·6·3	Not Out	3 1
Hammond :	6	Bowled	6
Sobers :	6·1	Not Out	7
Extras :	3		3
Total (3 wickets)			8 6

Grace scored first and, since it was a 1, Hutton became the batsman. He scored a 6 before being bowled. Bradman came in, and was the batsman for the last three balls of the over, scoring a 6, a 4 and a 4. At the end of the first over, Grace became the batsman but scored a 3, making Bradman become the batsman again.

Bradman scores a 6 and a 1, passing the batting back to Grace who scores a 4 and a 6. On the last throw of the over he gets a 3 so that he stays as the scoring batsman. On the second throw of the new over he gets a 3, which passes the scoring to Bradman. The next throw is a 5 (an appeal against Bradman) but it is a no ball and they score 3. This is written down opposite 'extras' and Grace becomes the scoring batsman again. Because of the no ball the next throw is the third of the over. He gets a 3, Bradman gets a 1 and Grace gets a 6 before being out on the last throw of the over.

The next batsman is Hammond but Bradman is the scoring batsman at the beginning of the new over. He gets a 6 and a 3, Hammond then gets a 6 at the third throw and is out on the fourth. The new batsman, Sobers, gets a 6 and a 1 from the last two throws. He would be the scoring batsman if the game continued.

As it is, three people are out and the score is 86 for 'three wickets'.

CRAG** *Two or more players (becomes slow with more than six)*

A splendid game which needs some preparation before it can be played properly. Together with *Yacht* some people think this is one of the best dice games.

You need three dice to play *Crag*.

To begin the game each player throws the three dice and the player with the highest score is the leader.

The leader throws the three dice again. He is trying to score points by making the numbers on the dice form one of the patterns described below and to do this is allowed to have one more throw of as many of the dice as he likes. When he has had both his throws any score he has made is written down on a special chart you have drawn and he passes the dice to the player on his left. This player makes his two throws and passes the dice on. And so on round the table.

The patterns which you are trying to make are:

1. *Ones* (only the 1s score – two 1s score 2 points).

2. *Twos* (only the 2s score – three 2s score 6 points).
3. *Threes* (only the 3s score – two 3s score 6 points).
4. *Fours* (only the 4s score – three 4s score 12 points).
5. *Fives* (only 5s score – two 5s score 10 points).
6. *Sixes* (only the 6s score – three 6s score 18 points).
7. *Odd Straight* (1–3–5 – scores 20 points).
8. *Even Straight* (2–4–6 – scores 20 points).
9. *Low Straight* (1–2–3 – scores 20 points).
10. *High Straight* (4–5–6 – scores 20 points).
11. *Three of a Kind* (all three dice the same – scores 25 points).
12. *Thirteen* – no doubles (3–4–6 or 2–5–6 – scores 26 points).
13. *Crag* (Thirteen with a double – 1–6–6, 3–5–5 or 4–4–5. This scores 50 points).

Each player throws all three dice on his turn and he can use the dice as thrown or can throw one, two or even

	Margaret	Veronica	Francis	Rosemary
Ones				
Twos				
Threes				
Fours				
Fives				
Sixes				
Odd Straight				
Even Straight				
Low Straight				
High Straight				
Three of a kind				
Thirteen				
Crag				
Totals				

all three of them for a second turn. He then chooses which pattern he wants to score under and, once he has chosen and the score has been written down, it cannot be altered. If a player can only score in one pattern he must choose that pattern. If he can score in more than one pattern he can choose whichever one he likes. If he cannot score in any pattern, he must choose which pattern he will leave blank.

It is easiest to write the scores in a chart with the names of the patterns down one side and the names of the players in order of play across the top as in the diagram.

The last seven patterns are the most difficult to throw and it is a good idea to aim for them at the beginning. As with *Yacht* great skill is needed in choosing which die or dice to set aside so that your score will be as high as possible. For example, a throw of 1–4–6 could become an Even Straight or a High Straight if the 1 is thrown. Or the 4 could be thrown, trying for a Crag. If you got this throw near the beginning of the game it would probably be best to try for Crag even though you have less chance of making it, but you will have to make up your mind in each case.

When all the players have filled in all thirteen spaces on the chart, with blanks if necessary, the scores are added up and the player with the largest total is the winner.

YACHT* *Two or more players (becomes very slow with more than six)*

Although this game may appear difficult at first sight it is really quite simple to play and can be very exciting. Some people think that *Yacht* and *Crag* are the two best dice games.

If you do want to play you must have five ordinary dice. It is just as well to allow enough time as well. This does not mean that the game is slow but there is so much to do when playing it that it can take a long time.

The players each throw the five dice and remember their own totals. The player with the highest total is the leader.

The leader throws the five dice again. He is trying to score points by making the numbers on the dice form the patterns shown below and to do this is allowed to have two more throws but can use as many dice for these throws as he likes. When he has made his three throws his score is written down on a chart which you draw and his turn has ended. He passes the dice to the next player on his left who makes three throws in his turn and passes the dice to his left, and so on round the table.

The patterns which each player is trying to make the dice show are:

1. *Ones* (only the 1s score – if he throws two 1s, he gets 2 points).
2. *Twos* (only the 2s score – three 2s score 6 points).
3. *Threes* (only the 3s score – two 3s score 6 points).
4. *Fours* (only the 4s score – four 4s score 16 points).
5. *Fives* (only the 5s score – six 5s score 30 points).
6. *Sixes* (only the 6s score – four 6s score 24 points).
7. *Little Straight* (1–2–3–4–5 – scores pip value 15 points and you can only score if the five dice show all these values).
8. *Big Straight* (2–3–4–5–6 – scores pip value 20 points; nothing else scores).
9. *Full House* (three numbers of one kind and two of another – for example three 3s and two 6s; the score is the total pip value – in this case 21 points).
10. *Four of a Kind* (four of any one number – scores the pip value of the four dice, four 5s scoring 20 points).
11. *Choice* (the player tries to score as many points as possible, there is no need to make a pattern; the score is the total pip value – 6–6–6–4–1 scores 23 points).
12. *Yacht* (all five dice showing the same number; you score the total pip value).

Before you begin to play draw up a chart like the one in the diagram on the next page with the names of the patterns down one side and the names of the players, in their order of throwing, across the top. Choose one of the players to keep the score and give him the chart.

As we have already said each player on his turn throws the five dice on to the table. He then chooses one of the five patterns and says its name out loud so that the scorer can hear it. He is not allowed to choose the same pattern twice. Only after he has said which pattern he is trying for is the player allowed to take his other two turns at throwing the dice.

	Margaret	Veronica	Francis	Rosemary
Ones				
Twos				
Threes				
Fours				
Fives				
Sixes				
Little Straight				
Big Straight				
Full House				
Four of a Kind				
Choice				
Yacht				
Totals				

Choosing which pattern to go for introduces the idea of skill and a player's cleverness in choosing properly counts for as much as his good luck in throwing. Since each group scores differently and the score depends on the number of pips on the dice, with five 1s scoring 5 points but five 6s scoring 30 points, you have to be careful to choose the pattern which will give you the greatest score. Since you can only use each pattern once you also have to choose between making small, certain scores, and trying for the larger ones with the risk of not scoring anything at all.

Once a player has thrown the five dice and named the pattern he is going for, he has to make another choice. This time he has to choose which dice to leave and which to throw again. He puts the dice he wants to keep to one side and throws the remainder on to the table. He can then put any of the dice he has just thrown over beside the dice he kept from his first throw. If this still leaves him with some dice he can throw these again for his third and final throw. All the dice are then gathered together and his score is calculated. Of course, a player can decide not to throw any more dice after either his first or second throw and this ends his turn. His score is calculated and the dice are passed on to the next player.

Suppose a player threw 2–2–2–3–3 on his first throw. He might call 'Full House', throw no more dice and score 12 points. He might, however, call 'Twos' and put the three 2s to one side, throwing the remaining dice to try to get more 2s. If the second throw does give him a 2 he puts it with the other three dice and throws the remaining die for his third, and final, turn. Of course, if the second throw does not produce any 2s, he will throw both the dice for his last throw. Because he has decided to go for Twos the player knows that he is sure to score 6 points and may get 8 or 10.

Instead of trying for Twos he could also try for Four of a Kind. Again he will keep the three 2s but if he does not throw another 2 in the next two throws he will score nothing. Even if he throws two 2s he will only score 8 points for the Four of a Kind.

When a player chooses Pattern 11, Choice, he throws the dice three times as before, but he scores the total value of all the face-up sides when he has finished his turn – the dice do not have to make any particular pattern.

Play goes on round the table with each player choosing one of the twelve patterns on each turn until they have all chosen all of them. The scores are then added up and the player who has the largest total is the winner.

As a matter of strategy it is a good idea to aim for Yacht, the two Straights, Four of a Kind, and Full House early on in the game since they are the hardest to throw.

Some players prefer to score the Little Straight and the Big Straight as 30 points each and Yacht at 50 points instead of at pip value. This does have some merit since they are very difficult to throw and should score accordingly.

LIAR DICE**   *Three or more players (four to six is best)*

Liar Dice is thought by some experts to be one of the best dice games and it certainly is one of the most interesting to play.

To play it you should have a set of poker dice – special dice which have pictures of playing cards on their faces and not spots. The cards usually chosen are the 9, 10, jack, queen, king and ace. There are five dice in a poker dice set.

You can use five ordinary dice if you like but you will find that the game is easier with poker dice.

You also need to know the different patterns you try to get on the dice – and their different values. These are given in the table below with the lowest first. (These are not in the same order as the hands in poker played with cards because the chances of getting them on the dice are different.)

1. *No pairs* – the value of the highest die is the value of the throw. 9–J–Q–K–A is 'ace high' – that is it has the value of the ace.

2. *Pair* – two 9s is below two 10s, two jacks, two queens, two kings and lastly two aces. No other combinations count.

3. *Two pairs* – four of the dice making two pairs of the same value. The higher pair gives the value of the hand. For example, two 9s, two 10s and a jack is beaten by two 9s, two jacks and a 10.

4. *Three* – three 9s is beaten by three 10s, three jacks, three queens, three kings and lastly three aces.

5. *Full House* – two dice of one kind and three of another – three 9s, two aces. The value of the three determines the value of the hand.

6. *Straight* – the dice in order of value. 9–10–J–Q–K is beaten by 10–J–Q–K–A.

7. *Four of a kind* – four dice of the same value. Four 9s is the lowest and four aces is the highest.

8. *Five of a kind* – all five dice of the same value. Five 9s is the lowest, five aces is the highest.

At the beginning of the game each player is given three counters (or matches). These count as lives and when a player has lost all three he is dead and can take no further part in the game.

When only one player has any lives left he is the winner.

The players each throw the dice once and the player who throws the highest 'hand' – that is, pattern on his five dice – is the first player.

He throws the dice on to the table, shielding them carefully with his left hand so that the other players cannot see their tops. He then names a hand – it need not be the same as the hand he has thrown.

The next player on his left may accept the call or challenge it. If it is accepted the dice, still hidden, are passed from the first player to the second. This player can then throw as many dice as he likes – but he must say how many he is going to throw (and he must always tell the truth about the number). He keeps all the dice hidden from the other players at all times. After he has thrown the selected number of dice, the second player must name a score which is higher than the one he accepted. If one player has only named a kind of hand – for example, Two Pairs – it counts as a higher hand to name particular values – for example, Two Pairs, kings high, or Two Pairs, queens on 9s. Once a particular value has been called the next player can either call a higher particular hand, or a higher kind of hand.

When the second player has made his call, the next player on his left can accept the hand or challenge it.

The dice pass round the table in this way, being hidden at all times, until one player challenges the call of the player before him.

On the challenge the dice are exposed, so that all players can see them. If the caller has named a hand that is smaller than or equal to the hand on the dice, the challenger loses a life. If the caller has named a hand greater than the hand shown on the dice, then the caller loses a life.

For example, suppose Margaret, Veronica, Francis and Rosemary are playing *Liar Dice*.

Margaret starts and throws Q–Q–Q–K–10. She calls 'A Pair', and Veronica accepts the call.

Veronica says 'Throwing two', throws two dice secretly and ends up with Q–Q–Q–K–9. She calls 'Threes' and Francis accepts it.

Francis says, 'Throwing two', and gets Q–Q–Q–K–10. He calls 'Three queens' and Rosemary accepts.

Rosemary says, 'Throwing two', and gets Q–Q–Q–9–10. She calls 'Four' and Margaret challenges.

The dice are revealed and are seen to be less than Rosemary's call. She loses a life and Margaret (sitting on her left) begins the next round.

5 PENCIL AND PAPER GAMES

You do not *have* to have a pencil and paper to play these games – they could be played perfectly well in the sand at the seaside using a stick to scratch the marks. Most of the games are easier to play with pencil and paper, however, although *Hackenbush* and *Sprouts* are best with chalk and a blackboard. Squared paper (if you can get some) is very useful for games like *Battleships*.

BOXES *Two to four players (best for two)*

This is a splendidly ingenious game for two players but three or four can play it although it is not so good.

Mark out a number of dots on a piece of paper so that they are at the corners of little squares. They do not have to make a big square or rectangle but they are usually drawn like that.

You can make the pattern as large as you like but, for two players, a square of seven or eight dots to each side does not make the game too long.

The players take it in turns to join pairs of dots which are next to each other, with a straight line going up and down or from side to side, as in the diagram.

The object of the game is to try to finish a little square by drawing its fourth side when the other three sides have already been drawn. Whenever a player does this he marks the square with his initial so that everybody knows that it is his.

When all the little squares have been completed and claimed by one or the other of the players the game ends.

The winner is the player who has got his initial in most little squares.

It is usual to let a player who finishes a square draw another line in the same turn. This means that his turn does not end until he draws a line which does not finish a

square. In the diagram below R has won 9 squares to M's 11. Notice that, whoever plays next, the turn after that can fill in all the remaining squares on the board.

R	R	M	M	M
R	R	R	M	M
M	M	M	R	M
R	R	R	M	M

THE WORM   *Two to four players (two is best)*

Just as for *Boxes* you start this game by marking out a pattern of dots at the corners of squares. You can use any number of dots you like but it is best if you make them into either a square or a rectangle.

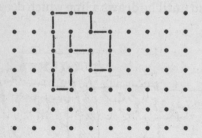

One of the players is chosen to start and he joins any two dots which are next to each other with a straight line. The next player must draw a straight line from one of the ends of this line to one of the dots next to it. Each player, in turn, joins on to one end of the line.

The loser is the first player to join on to the line itself.

In the diagram below, of a game between two players, the first player has lost because his next line must join on to the 'worm'.

SQUARES IN LINE* *Two players*

This game is very like *Boxes* but you start out with all the squares drawn in to make a big square. When you play this game for the first time you should use a big square with six or seven squares on each side. But as you get better at playing you can make the square bigger.

It is a good idea to use graph paper for this game but you could play on a squared board, putting counters on the squares instead of writing on them.

The players take it in turn to mark one little square. Whenever the little square is the last one in a line, either from side to side, or up and down, or diagonally, he is given a score equal to the number of squares in the line. If more than one line is completed by a player he scores points for all the squares in all the lines.

The player who finishes a line is given an extra turn and therefore his turn ends when he cannot complete any more lines.

The winner is the player who, when all the squares have been filled in, has scored most points.

It is important to remember in playing this game that most squares have four lines running through them (one across, one up and down, one sloping up to the right and one sloping down to the right). Watch out for a chance to score from more than one of these lines.

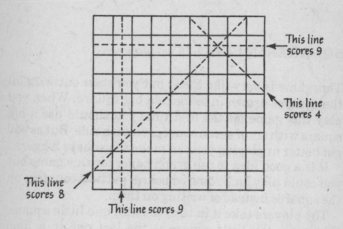

This line scores 9

This line scores 4

This line scores 8

This line scores 9

COL* *Two or more players*

Another game invented by Colin Vout, *Col* is a map-colouring game which was originally meant for two players. It can be played by as many people as you can provide with coloured pens or pencils.

In the ordinary two-person game, you start by drawing a map – both players can join in for this and you just have to make sure that all the 'countries' are separate.

The two players need pens of different colours, say Red and Blue.

To start the game, Blue colours any country he likes. Red then colours any country he chooses and so on, with the two players taking turns to colour countries. The only rule is that no two countries which touch along a line can have the same colour.

The winner is the last player to be able to colour a country.

When more than two people play, they each have pens of different colours and take it in turns to colour the map. A player who cannot go drops out and the others carry on until only one is left and he is the winner.

SPROUTS* *Two players*

This magnificent game was invented in 1967 by two mathematicians at Cambridge and it has since sprouted round the world.

The game starts with any number of dots on a sheet of paper – at first it is best to use only three or four dots.

The players take it in turns to draw a line joining any two dots, or joining a dot to itself. When he has done this the player puts a new dot on the line he has just drawn. It is then the other player's turn.

When you are drawing a line you must not let it cross itself, nor any line that has been drawn already, nor must it go through a dot. You must also remember that each dot can only have up to three lines leaving it.

The winner is the last player to be able to draw a line. The game can also be played so that the winner is the first player who cannot go on his turn.

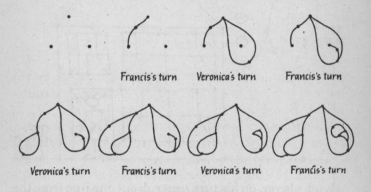

Francis's turn   Veronica's turn   Francis's turn

Veronica's turn   Francis's turn   Veronica's turn   Francis's turn

Veronica cannot go. Francis wins.

HACKENBUSH* *Two players*

This game can be played using pencil and paper but it is probably easier to use a blackboard and chalk since you have to rub out the lines.

The idea of the game is that you draw a picture of anything you like but the ends of each line must be clearly marked. The normal way of doing this is to mark each crossing point with a small dot, as in the diagram. The line across the bottom is not counted as part of the picture but dots are put on it also, as shown.

Each player, on his turn, can rub out one line from the picture. A line only goes from one dot to the next. After a player has had his turn any lines not connected to the ground are also rubbed out (because anything not connected to the ground falls down). So, if the first player rubs out the trunk of the tree, then all the branches and

the apples will also be rubbed out. Of course, if he only takes an apple, the rest will stand.

Rubbing out the left-hand wall of the house does not make it collapse, since the roof is connected to the ground by the right-hand wall.

The last player to be able to rub out a line is the winner and it is usual to let the *loser* draw the picture for the next game.

This game looks extremely simple but it has been studied by many mathematicians, including John Horton Conway, who has worked out a complete theory of how to play it.

BATTLESHIPS* *Two players*

This is a splendid game for two players which can be made as easy or as difficult as you please. The only problem is that you need to draw a new board for each game but this is quite easily done with a rule and pencil. You could use printed graph paper (some of which has quite large squares) or you can buy pads that have been printed with the squares you need.

Each player needs to draw two large squares, each ten squares by ten squares. In one of them he will put his own fleet of battleships, in the other square he will show where he has fired shots at the enemy and which ships he has found. Of course, neither player lets the other one see where he has put his own battleships.

	A	B	C	D	E	F	G	H	I	J
1									S	
2		B			C	C	C			
3		B							C	
4		B			D	D			C	
5		B							C	
6				S			D	D		
7		D							S	
8		D		D	D		S			
9										
10		S		S						

	A	B	C	D	E	F	G	H	I	J
1										
2										
3										
4										
5										
6										
7										
8										
9										
10										

The fleet belonging to each player is made up of one battleship (shown as one little square wide and four long; each little square marked B); two cruisers (one little square wide and three long; each little square marked C); four destroyers (one little square wide and two long; each little square marked D); and six submarines (each one little square marked S). The ships can be put anywhere you like on the big square, up and

down or across – but not diagonally. The ships must not touch each other even at a corner. If you look at the diagram you will see one way you can put out your ships.

You will see that in the diagram the letters A to J are written across the top, and the numbers 1 to 10 written down one side. This lets the players name each little square by giving its letter and number. For example, squares B10, D6 and G8 have submarines on them (go along the top until you come to column B and then go down the column until you come to row 10; and so on). Squares B2, B3, B4 and B5 have the battleship on them.

When the players have each put out their ships on one of the big squares they have drawn (without letting each other see, of course) the first player chooses a square and calls out its letter and number, E5 say. The second player then says 'Nothing' if he does not have a ship on that square, or the name of a ship ('Cruiser' for example) if it has been a lucky choice. The first player then puts a cross on square E5 of his empty big square (if he got nothing) or writes the letter of the ship (if he got a hit). The second player puts a cross in that square of his ship square.

The second player then calls out a letter and a number, and the first player tells what he has hit, if anything. The second player then puts a cross or a ship letter in that square of his empty big square and the first player puts a cross in that square of his ship square.

Each player takes it in turn to fire a shot and makes a careful note of which ships he hits and where they are placed. After the game has been going for some time the empty square will begin to look like this

```
     A B C D E F G H I J
 1  |  |  |  |  |  |  |  |  |  |  |
 2  |⊗|  |⊗|  |  |  |  |  |  |  |
 3  |⊗|B |X |⊗|⊗|X |⊗|  |  |  |
 4  |⊗|B |X |⊗|D |D |⊗|  |  |  |
 5  |⊗|B |⊗|⊗|X |X |⊗|⊗|  |  |
 6  |⊗|  |⊗|S |⊗|D |D |⊗|  |  |
 7  |  |  |⊗|⊗|⊗|X |⊗|⊗|  |  |
 8  |  |  |  |  |  |  |  |  |  |  |
 9  |  |  |  |  |  |  |  |  |  |  |
10  |  |  |  |  |  |  |  |  |  |  |
```

Each × shows where a square has had nothing in it. The squares marked D, B or S show where destroyers, a submarine and part of a battleship have been hit. The squares marked ⊗ must be empty because ships are not allowed to touch each other and so, when a ship has been found, you know that all the squares next to it must be empty.

This player's next shot will be either B2 or B6 since either of them could hold the missing bit of battleship.

The game goes on until one player has managed to hit all the ships belonging to the other. He has sunk the enemy's fleet and is the winner.

You must be very careful to keep a note of which squares your opponent has chosen and which you have chosen. You must also be careful not to waste shots by choosing squares which you should know are empty since they are next to ships.

This way of playing *Battleships* is the very simplest but you can make it more difficult by letting each player have more than one shot but not telling him which one has hit a ship, if he has been lucky enough to get a hit. For example, if you are playing that you each have two shots at a time, your opponent could call out D4, E4 and you would tell him 'one hit on a destroyer'. He then has to try to work out which shot did the damage. Of course, you have to do some working out on your turn.

The game can be played like this, with two, three, four or five shots each on your turn, but it is probably best not to try to play with more than five shots.

Another way to play is to start with fewer ships – a battleship, a cruiser and two destroyers say – and four shots each. Whenever a ship is completely destroyed the player to whom it belongs loses a shot. This continues until one player has lost all four ships.

You do not have to play *Battleships* with the size of fleet I have described. You could have more ships, or fewer. You could introduce other kinds of ships – marking four squares in a two by two square with the letter A for aircraft carrier. You could have one atom bomb each in each game which could be let off by a player whenever he liked. (The best way of doing this is to say 'Atom bomb on square F6' and any ships on that square or the eight squares surrounding it are counted as being destroyed. Of course, you do not have to say F6.)

You can also play *Battleships* on larger squares than ten by ten but, before you make the board too big, be careful that you have enough time to finish the game.

BLACK* *Two players*

This very simple, but intriguing, game was invented by a student called William Black some years ago, but it has not been described very often.

To start you draw a pattern of squares – this can be either a rectangle or a square, and can be as big as you like. It is probably best to use a big square with eight little squares on each side for playing but I shall only use a four-by-four-square square to explain the game.

You shade the bottom right-hand corner of the board – this is the square you are trying to get to.

In the game each player, on his turn, is allowed to draw one of the three marks shown below in one of the little squares. At least one part of his mark must join on to the path that has already been made.

The first player must put a cross in the top left-hand corner of the board but the second player can put any mark he likes so long as the path which is made by his mark joining on to the cross does not go to the edge of the board. (This means he cannot use the third of the diagrams above.)

If a player joins the path on to an edge he loses but if he joins it on to the shaded square he wins.

For example suppose two people are playing *Black*, the pattern could grow like this

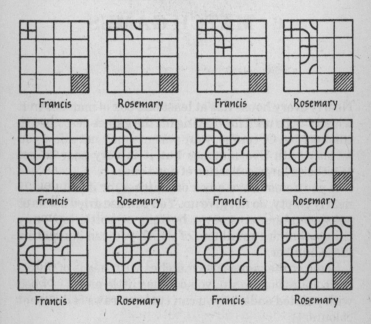

| Francis | Rosemary | Francis | Rosemary |

And Francis is forced to join the path on to the edge of the board on his next turn and he, therefore, loses.

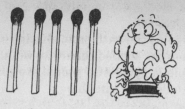

6 MATCH GAMES

Nearly every house has at least one box of matches in it
which can be used for playing all the games described in
this section. Of course, your parents may not allow you
to play with live matches but it is very easy to get
together a large collection of dead ones.

If you do not have a box of matches, or if your box is
nearly empty, do not give up. You can use dried beans or
peas, counters, or screws, buttons or bottle tops, any
things that are small and of which you can get quite a
large number.

Some of the games use matches with heads of different colours but, again, you can use little pieces of wood
with painted ends, or you can cut up straws of different
colours.

TAKE THE LAST *Two or more players*

This is a very simple game which young children enjoy.

You put out a lot of matches in a single pile on the
table. It does not matter how many matches you put out
but it is better to use about fifty.

Before you start taking matches, you agree on a number less than ten.

Each player then takes it in turn to take matches from the pile. At each turn you can take as many matches as you like but not more than the number you chose at the beginning.

The player who takes the last match is the winner.

Suppose fifty matches had been put in the pile and the number chosen by the players was six. The first player could take one, two, three, four, five or six matches. The second player on his turn could take any number from one to six inclusive.

You must take at least one match when it is your turn.

It is best not to choose a number that is too big – something between three and ten is probably best for fifty matches.

You can also play this game with more than two players, when it becomes more fun – especially if you play it so that the player who takes the last match is the loser. Let everybody start with three lives and lose a life every time they take the last match. The winner is the person who still has lives left when everybody else has lost all theirs.

KAYLES *Two players*

This game was invented by H. E. Dudeney, a famous inventor of puzzles and games, and it is a very interesting game for two.

Any number of matches are arranged in a long line. It is best not to use more than twenty because the game goes on for too long.

When it is your turn you can take either one match, or two matches which are touching each other. For example, if you have three matches touching each other

you could take the first two, or the last two, or any one of them on your turn. If you take the middle one your opponent can pick up only one of the two matches left, since they are not touching.

The winner is the player who takes the last match. You can also play this game so that the loser is the player who takes the last match.

NIM *Two players*

This is the most widely known of the match games and it is usually played by two. Three or more people can play but it becomes much more difficult.

The matches are arranged in separate piles – it does not matter how many piles you have, nor how many matches there are in each pile.

Each player, when it is his turn, takes as many matches as he likes from any one of the piles. He can take one match or the whole pile or any number in between just as he pleases.

This continues until there are no matches left.

The player who takes the last match (or the last pile) is the winner.

For example, suppose the piles are

A   B   C

and the players are Veronica and Francis. If Veronica takes one match from pile *C*, she leaves

A   B   C

Then if Francis takes all pile *B*, he leaves

Veronica now takes three matches from pile *C*, leaving

and if Francis takes two matches from pile *A*, he leaves

Veronica will take two matches from pile *C* to make

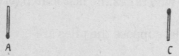

and Francis must pick up one of the matches, leaving the other for Veronica who will win since this is the last match.

Nim, like most of the other match games, can be played so that the person who picks up the last match is the loser but this does not really change the way the game is played.

In another variation of *Nim* the players choose a number (smaller than the number of piles) before any matches have been removed. A player can then, on his turn, take as many matches as he likes from any number of piles up to the chosen number (he must, of course, take the same number of matches from each pile).

Yet another variation allows a player to split a pile in two on his turn, instead of taking any matches. You can decide which rule will govern splitting before you start but it could be that you can only split piles which have an odd number of matches in them. Alternatively, you could arrange that only even piles could be split, or piles could only be split into unequal parts, or that piles could be split into as many parts as you like.

In all these different variations you can play either that the winner is the player who takes the last match or that the loser takes the last match.

TACTIX   *Two players*

This is the first of the match games which uses matches
spread out on the table to make a 'board' which is broken
up and taken away during the game. It was invented by
Piet Hein, who also made up the game of *Hex*.

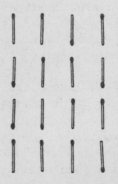

In *Tactix* the matches (or counters) are laid out to make a square or rectangle which can be as big as you like.

The two players take it in turn to take as many matches as they like from any row or column *but* the matches must be next to each other.

For example, if the first player takes three matches from the third column

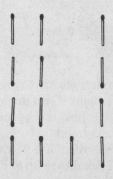

the second player cannot take the whole first row in one go because there is a gap in it. He can take the first two matches in it, if he wants to.

The second player could take all the matches in the fourth row if he wanted to because there are no gaps in it.

The players keep on taking matches in their turns until one of them picks up the last match. This player is the winner.

If you try to play *Tactix* with the rule that the loser is the player who takes the last match you may discover a simple way of playing which means that you never lose.

SPILLIKINS *Two or more players*

All the other games that we have described for matches need some thinking about if you are going to play them properly. *Spillikins* is just the opposite; it just needs carefulness and steady hands.

Put all the matches from a box into an egg cup – it doesn't matter if the heads are up or down.

The first player takes one match out of the egg cup and lays it across the top of the other matches in the egg cup. The other players do exactly the same when it is their turn, so that the matches gradually get piled higher and higher across the rest. And the rest keep on getting smaller in number.

If you are unlucky enough to knock some matches down, so that they fall on the table, you have to keep them until the end of the game.

The winner is the player with the fewest matches when all the matches have been taken out of the egg cup and laid across the top.

7 OTHER GAMES

A handful of games which do not need any special
equipment and can be played almost anywhere.
Favourites with many children, they are only put
together here because they do not fit into any categories.
They are just good games.

SPOOF* *Three or more players (best with six)*

A very enjoyable game of bluff which will soon teach you
when someone else is lying and when they are not.

All you need to play the game is three small objects for
each player – coins, counters, pebbles, matches – anything that will fit easily into the palm of the hand and be
hidden with the closed fingers.

The point of the game is to guess the total number of
objects that have been hidden by all the players.

After one of the players has been chosen to start, by
counting or cutting cards or tossing coins, each player
chooses the number of objects he will hide in his fist. He,
therefore, puts that number secretly into his hand,

closes his hand and holds his closed fist out in front of him so that all the other players can see it.

When all the players have put out their fists, the first player guesses how many objects in all will appear on opening all the fists. If six people are playing, the number might be anything from nothing (six empty hands) to eighteen (six hands with three objects each). If four people are playing, the number could be anything from nothing to twelve.

Once the first player has made a guess the player on his left can say what he thinks the number will be – but no two players can choose the same number.

The players take it in turns to call their guesses, moving round to the left all the time, until everybody has spoken. Then all the fists are opened and the total number of objects for that round is discovered.

The player who called the correct total, or got nearest, drops out.

For the next round the player on the original first player's left has the first call. This continues until only one player is left and he is the loser of the game.

The first player has the advantage that he can call any number he likes but, by calling, he tells the other players something about how many objects he has hidden. For example, suppose five people are playing (with the possible totals going from nought to fifteen) and the first player calls, 'Twelve'. The other players will then guess that he has got three objects in his hand. If the second player has three in *his* hand he will probably guess high too, say 'Thirteen' and this tells the other three players that he has hidden a lot of objects in his hand.

As you will see this means that the last player in each round can get a very good idea of how many objects are out by the time it comes round to his turn to guess. Of course, he may not be able to say the correct number because it has already been chosen by another player. This explains why it is important to change the first player for each round.

It is a good idea to mislead the other players occasionally by calling a low total when you have three objects in your hand, or a high one when you have chosen no objects. Do not do this too often, however, because everyone will suspect your bluff.

HANGMAN*   *Two or more players*

This is an excellent game which deserves its wide popularity. It can be played by two or more people but if more than six play it is best to divide them into two groups which play against each other. If three, four or five are playing they must take turns in calling out the letters.

One player thinks of a word and draws a row of dashes, one for each letter of the word. The other players take turns in guessing the letters of the secret word, usually starting with the vowels since there must be one of them in it. If the guessed letter is in the word it is written over the correct dash of the row. If the letter appears more than once then all the places where it occurs must be filled in.

Most of the time, of course, the guessed letter will not be in the secret word and part of a gallows is drawn for each incorrect guess. The object of the game is to guess the word before the gallows and the man on it are completed.

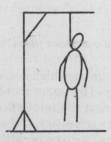

The gallows shown allows the player to make thirteen incorrect guesses before he is 'hanged'. This number can easily be made larger, if you want to make it a bit easier to find the word, or smaller, if you want to make it harder. You do this by changing the way you draw the gallows or the man. Some people start with the gallows complete and you only have six chances before being 'hanged'. Others say you must add fingers, feet, eyes, nose, mouth and hair.

When playing with young children it is a good idea to write down the letters as they guess them so that they can see whether they have had a letter before or not.

GHOSTS AND SUPERGHOSTS** *Three or more players (best with four, five or six)*

Superghosts is probably one of the best spelling games that you can play. Its rules are very similar to those of *Ghosts* and it is obvious that someone had the bright idea that a good game (*Ghosts*) would become a splendid game (*Superghosts*) by a very small change in the rules.

To play *Ghosts* the players sit in a circle – it does not have to be a real circle so long as everybody knows who plays before him and after him. The first player, who is chosen by cutting a pack of cards or tossing coins, names a letter. For example, 'C'.

The second player, thinking of a word beginning with that letter, names the second letter. For example, 'A', thinking of the word 'CAb'.

Since the object of the game is *not* to be the one to finish a word, and since you are not allowed to finish a word of three letters in *Ghosts*, the third player has to add a letter which will not spell a word but which will be the first three letters of a real word. Usually he will try to think of a letter which will force the next player to finish a word. The third player in our example tries 'V', making 'CAV'.

You are not allowed to finish a word of three letters or more. If you do finish a word, any other player can call 'That's a word' and, if they are right, you get a black

mark. If they are wrong, they get a black mark.

When you have collected three black marks you become a ghost and cannot take any further part in the game.

In our example the fourth player has to add a letter to 'CAV' and try not to finish a word. He will quickly realize that he can add 'A' (thinking of 'cavalcade', 'cavalier', or 'cavalry') or 'I' (thinking of 'caviare', 'cavil' or 'cavity') or 'O' (thinking of 'cavort'). For each of these possibilities he will count round the circle to see where they could end. Of course, he will not choose letters which can spell words which end on himself.

Whenever a player hesitates too long, the preceding player can call out, 'Add or challenge'. One minute is then allowed for the player to add a letter or to challenge the preceding player. You challenge the player before you when you think he has made a spelling mistake or is not really spelling a word. Suppose you were the fourth player and the third player had just added 'Z' to 'SY' making 'SYZ'. You might challenge, thinking there was no word beginning like this, only to be told 'Syzygy'. In that case you would get a black mark. But if the player before you had made a mistake, or was just bluffing, he would get a black mark.

When a word is ended, or a challenge has been made, the next player starts the next round by naming a letter.

The game ends when all the players except one have become ghosts and he is the winner.

In *Superghosts*, letters can be added before or after those which have already been named. For example, the sequence of letters might go: 'C', 'A after' (CA), 'N before' (NCA), 'P after' (NCAP), 'A after' (NCAPA) and so on – until it spells 'incapable' or something else.

The only other change in the rules for *Superghosts* is that three-letter words are allowed but if you complete a word of four or more letters you get a black mark.

In both *Ghosts* and *Superghosts* it is important to count round the circle before you name a letter to see where a word will end. It is also best to count after other people have called letters since you may have to think of a way of not ending a word on your turn.

It is best not to use proper names, abbreviations or foreign words in either game. And you should have a good dictionary handy to settle arguments.

INDEX

ALL THE YEAR ROUND
Toni Arthur

Can you make yourself invisible? Do you know the best thing to do with old socks? What's the secret of making exploding snacks? How can you keep witches away? If you don't know the answers to any of these questions, you must read this book. TV presenter and singer Toni Arthur has compiled an incredible variety of traditional customs and stories, songs and games to keep you occupied and interested during even the greyest times of the year. The activities range from the very simple, requiring only a pencil and paper, to the more complicated which may require help from adults.

GO! A BOOK OF GAMES
Philippa Dickinson

Worried about your party and how you're going to entertain your guests? Your worries are over. Covering the spectrum from silent to riotous, and useful for children of seven upwards, this selection of games will make any party a howling success.

THE ANIMAL QUIZ BOOK
Sally Kilroy

Why do crocodiles swallow stones? Which bird migrates the furthest? Can kangaroos swim? With over a million species, the animal kingdom provides a limitless source of fascinating questions, and Sally Kilroy has assembled a feast for enquiring minds from Domestic Animals to Dinosaurs, Fish to Footprints, and Reptiles to Record Breakers. Discover where creatures live, how they adapt to their conditions, the way they treat each other, the dangers they face – you will be amazed at how much you *didn't* know!

Johnny Ball's
THINK BOX

Television personality Johnny Ball, whose TV shows have made maths a popular subject again with millions of children, shares his enthusiasm for numbers in this fascinating book of puzzles, tricks and brain teasers. Find out about Russian multiplication, the Chinese abacus, Rubik's cube and magic squares. Learn how to do the four-suit swindle and the six-card trick. Discover how to make a Möbius Band and a tetraflexagon . . .

CODES FOR KIDS
Neil Burton Jr.

Crammed full with a fascinating range of codes and ciphers, all easily coded and yet nearly impossible to break, here is the ideal way to keep prying eyes away from your secrets. It is an indispensable handbook for secret agents, generals on the battle-field, high-powered executives, clubs, friends, and anybody with a taste for skulduggery and intrigue.

CHIPS, COMPUTERS AND ROBOTS
Judy Allen

A straightforward, fascinating explanation of microtechnology. With large clear illustrations this book will be of great interest to readers of all ages, including adults, who would like to know more about microchips and their use.

THE PUFFIN BOOK OF CAR GAMES
Douglas St. P. Barnard

Long car journeys can be boring, hot and tiring, and it helps if you know lots of games to play that will keep your mind (or your fingers) occupied. There are over a hundred car games, none of which needs anything more complex than a box of matches, a map, a pencil or a piece of paper. There are also games to play outside the car, when you stop for a picnic, perhaps, or when you are spending the day on the beach. In fact, not only is it a book to make the going great – it will also help you enjoy being there!

MICRO GAMES
Patrick Bossert and Philippa Dickinson

Patrick Bossert (of *You Can do The Cube*) has turned his attention to the micro-computer and devised a great collection of games listings. There is a death-defying bomb run, a hair-raising car race, a bat-and-ball game, fiendish puzzles to work out, and many more. All the games require lightning reactions, quick thinking or good powers of observation. All will give hours of fun – and all will help you understand your computer that little bit better!

THE CALENDAR QUIZ BOOK
Barbara Gilgallon and Sue Samuels

A quiz book with a difference that will baffle, stimulate and entertain readers of 10 to 14. Divided into twelve sections, one for each month of the year, it has over 1,000 questions on an enormous variety of topics – anything from the inventor of television to the August Bank Holiday. Ideal for use alone, with family or friends, at home or at school.

MY SECRET FILE
John Astrop

A cross between a file, a diary and a suggestions book. Organised on a loose chronological basis, it consists of various questionnaires, personal quizzes and tables to be filled in. Sample subjects include an IF page (If I could live anywhere, I'd live ...) and a Christmas Presents page (got what? gave what?). And there's a sequel: DEEPER SECRETS, for even more secret secrets!

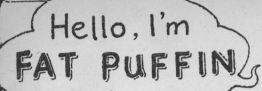